Fruitcakes and Holiday Caskets

A Down South Café Mystery

Gayle Leeson

Grace Abraham Publishing
Bristol, Virginia

Gayle Leeson/Grace Abraham Publishing
13335 Holbrook Street, Suite 10
Bristol, Virginia 24202
www.gayleleeson.com

Publisher's Note: This is a work of fiction. Names, characters, places, and incidents are a product of the author's imagination. Locales and public names are sometimes used for atmospheric purposes. Any resemblance to actual people, living or dead, or to businesses, companies, events, institutions, or locales is completely coincidental.

Cover design by Wicked Smart Designs.

Book Layout ©2017 BookDesignTemplates.com

Ordering Information:
Quantity sales. Special discounts are available on quantity purchases by corporations, associations, and others. For details, contact the "Special Sales Department" at the address above.

Fruit Baskets and Holiday Caskets/Gayle Leeson. -- 1st ed.
ISBN 978-1-7320195-3-9

Dedicated to Tim, Lianna, and Nicholas

Chapter One

"**G**oodbye, Amy. You've been such a sweet girl to me, and I want you to know how much I love you. I'm hanging up and calling Jackie now. I want her to be the last one who hears my voice."

Before I could say a word, Aunt Bess hung up. I knew I'd better call Mom and find out what was going on. We were in the midst of a severe thunderstorm—strange for December, but not unheard of—and our power was out. I took my lit candle into the kitchen to retrieve my phone from my purse. Rory, my little brown terrier, followed me, his toenails clicking on the tile floor. Princess Eloise, my—or, rather, Mom's—white Persian cat, remained on the armchair and flicked her tail.

Calling Mom's number as I walked back to the living room, I sank onto the sofa. Rory hopped onto my lap, his body trembling as a clap of thunder rattled the windows.

"Amy, is everything all right down there?" Mom asked in lieu of a greeting.

"You tell me. Aunt Bess just called to say goodbye. She's probably talking with Jackie now because she wants her granddaughter to be the last one who hears her voice."

"Oh, good grief."

"Is she sick?" I asked.

"No, but I'm about to kill her." Mom growled in frustration. "I'll call you back as soon as I try to keep her from scaring Jackie half to death."

Mom ended the call, and I cuddled Rory and wondered what Aunt Bess was up to now. To call Aunt Bess eccentric would be a kind under-statement. She was actually my great-aunt—my grandmother's sister. Before Nana died, Aunt

Bess moved into the "big house" with her. Mom and I lived in a smaller house down the hill from Nana's place. And after Nana died, Mom moved in with Aunt Bess to take care of her and to make sure she didn't get into any mischief. Well, the latter turned out to be a lost cause.

When my phone rang approximately ten minutes later, it was Mom informing me that "Henny Penny thinks the sky is falling."

I had guessed Aunt Bess was making something out of nothing, but I waited for Mom to elaborate.

"The roof over her bed is leaking. A few drops of water plunked her on the forehead, and she became convinced that the roof was about to fall in on top of her." Mom blew out a breath. "And, naturally, instead of getting up like a normal person, she began phoning in her goodbyes."

Laughing, I said, "I'm glad it's nothing serious."

"Well, unfortunately, I'm afraid it might be more significant than I let on to Aunt Bess. Jackie said she'll send Roger over tomorrow morning to assess the damage. I've moved Aunt Bess's bed and put a bucket under the leak, and I'm going to get Aunt Bess settled into the guest room. Wish me luck."

"I'd be happy to slip on my raincoat and come help out if you need me," I said.

"Please don't. I don't want to have to worry about your being struck by lightning on your way here. Besides, I'm sure the pets are frightened and need you there."

"That's true." I gave Rory a reassuring pat. "Still, I'll come up before I go to work in the morning."

"With the way this night is going, that'll probably be about the time I fall asleep," Mom said. "Would you mind dropping in *after* work?"

"Sure. I'll bring dinner. Just call me if you need anything before then."

As soon as I arrived at the café the next morning, I got the coffee brewing. I was going to need plenty of caffeine today to keep me moving. Our electricity had come back on at around eleven o'clock. I'd gotten up and looked up the hill toward the big house and saw lights on in the living room, so I was reassured the power was back on there too. I wasn't worried so much about the lights, but I didn't want the heat to be out for very long. Mom had gas logs in the fireplace in the living room—maybe she'd bundled Aunt Bess up, and the two of them had sat in the living room until the electricity was restored.

Jackie was yawning as she walked through the door, so I knew she was probably as tired as I. "Coffee?"

Nodding, I raised my cup. "I have the French vanilla, but there's a pot of dark roast that should be finished brewing by now."

My cousin poured herself a cup of the dark roast and came to stand beside me at the counter. "What are we doing just standing here?" she asked, knowing I should be halfway through the morning kitchen prep by now.

"Procrastinating?"

She nodded. "Works for me."

"What time did your lights come back on?"

"The power never went out in my building." She jerked her head toward the kitchen. "Was the power off here?"

"I don't think it was in the café. Ryan assured me the power hadn't been out in this part of town, and I was relieved to see that there weren't any fallen limbs or other debris on the road or in the parking lot."

"Roger is going by the big house to check on the roof this morning," Jackie said. "He'll be by here when he's finished."

"Good. I hope it's nothing major." I was interrupted by the phone ringing. I answered, "Down South Café, Amy speaking."

"Hi, darlin'. It's Dilly."

Dilly Boyd was almost always our first customer of the day. She rose with the sun and often dined with her beau Walter Jackson.

"How are you?" I asked.

"I'm fine, but I don't have heat at my house."

"Oh, no! Is your electricity still off?"

"No, just the heat pump," Dilly said. "I believe I've got on nearly every stitch of clothes I own."

"I'm so sorry! How can I help?"

"What is it?" Jackie whispered.

I held up an index finger as I listened to Dilly.

"Walter is coming by to pick up our breakfast. We'd both like the pancakes, eggs, and sausage. And don't forget the biscuit for the raccoon," she said. "I hope he weathered the storm all right."

The raccoon Dilly mentioned came down out of the woods behind her house every evening at dusk to get a biscuit. I didn't think Dilly considered the little masked bandit a pet, but she certainly looked out for him.

"We'll have your order ready for you when Walter gets here," I said. "Have you called someone about your heat pump?"

"No one is open for business yet," she said.

After telling her to let us know if there was any-thing—other than breakfast—we could do to help, I ended the call and started on her order. Scott and Luis, our waiter and busboy/dishwasher, arrived, and I could hear patrons begin to trickle into the dining room as I worked.

We had Christmas music playing softly, and I could catch snippets of tunes over the sounds of fry-ing sausage and clinking silverware. We had a small, decorated tree atop the display case, and there were garlands hung over the doors and windows. Hearing a bit of the chorus of *Silver Bells*, I hummed along as I flipped Dilly's pancakes.

Jackie was making a fresh batch of coffee when Roger came into the café with Devon, one of his crew members.

"Hey, guys," she said. "Are you hungry?"

"Always." Devon patted his stomach.

I went over to the window between the dining room and the kitchen. "How's the roof?"

"Not good, Flowerpot." Roger had given me the nickname when we were kids and had, unfortunately, never let it go. "Devon and I put a tarp over the end and weighted it down with bricks. We're going to get the materials to fix it as soon as we finish up here."

"Do you think the entire roof should be replaced, or just the damaged area?" I asked.

"It would be best to do it all." He accepted the cup of coffee Jackie sat in front of him. "Thanks, hon." Turning back to me, he said, "I'm afraid if we don't fix the entire thing, we'll just be repairing one section right after another."

I nodded. "Good thinking."

"What are you two wanting for breakfast?" Jackie asked.

"I'd love the Belgian waffles," Devon said, as he emptied a packet of sugar into his coffee.

"I'll have biscuits and eggs," Roger said.

"Oh, hey, you guys work on heat pumps, don't you?" I asked.

Roger groaned. "Don't tell me yours went out during the storm."

"Not mine—Dilly Boyd's. When I spoke with her, she was trying to find someone to answer her call."

"Everybody's swamped today." Devon turned to Roger. "Want me to give her a call?"

"Would you? If you could take care of that while I get the roofing materials for Amy's mom, that would be terrific."

I wrote Dilly's number on a napkin and slid it across the counter to Devon. "You're a lifesaver. I can't stand the thought of her being over there with no heat. I mean, it's not that cold right now—not to me, anyway—but..."

"But she needs to have her heat pump working," he finished. "I understand. And, Jackie, don't forget you're gonna help me with that thing we talked about."

She grinned. "I haven't forgotten."

When she followed me into the kitchen, I asked, "What thing are you helping Devon with?"

"Finding a Christmas present for his wife. He wants to get her a necklace similar to one her grandmother used to wear all the time. I'm scouring all the online vintage sites."

"Good luck."

She rolled her eyes. "Thanks. I need it. I didn't dream a comparable necklace could be so hard to find or be so expensive. That's probably why he was trying to make a deal for the cheaper appliances."

The phone rang, and I quickly put on my headset before answering. "Down South Café, Amy—"

"Don't buy any fruit for a while!" Mom exclaimed.

"Um...okay."

"Your Aunt Bess posted on social media that she might be dying, and four fruit baskets have already arrived, including a huge one from the fire department!"

"Why does Aunt Bess think she's dying?" I asked. "Does she still think the roof is going to cave in?"

"No. Either that few drops of rain that pelted her on the forehead and gave her a chill will likely result in pneumonia, or the rat droppings she found on her bed after she hopped out of it will probably result in her contracting rabies or the plague."

I went on into the kitchen to work on the breakfast orders. "Rat droppings?" I lowered my voice to almost a whisper so none of the café patrons would hear and think we had vermin.

"I should say not. They were pieces of chocolate cookie!" Mom gave a growl of frustration. "Aunt Bess knows good and well those were crumbs and not rat droppings. We both saw additional droppings and one leftover cookie on a saucer on her nightstand. She's just milking this entire ordeal, as she calls it, for all the attention she can get."

"And fruit," I added. "Any flowers?"

"Not yet."

I felt bad for Mom. Corralling Aunt Bess had become a twenty-four seven responsibility. After Nana died, Mom had given up her job and moved into the big house to care for Aunt Bess, and it was times like these when I realized how much of her freedom and independence Mom had sacrificed.

"I love you, Mom."

She chuckled. "Do I sound that pitiful?"

"Yes. If it helps, when I bring up dinner this evening, I'll make sure the dessert isn't chocolate. We don't want any more rat droppings around the house."

Gayle Leeson

"In the meantime, I'll try to keep Aunt Bess entertained and off the computer," Mom said.

After ending the call, Jackie wanted to know the question they'd overheard me ask Mom at the beginning of the call: Why did Aunt Bess think she was dying? I explained the situation to her as she helped me finish up the breakfast orders and Scott boxed up Dilly's and Walter's takeout.

"Would you mind if I visit Aunt Bess after work today?" Scott asked. "Having the roof get torn up probably scared her, and it sounds like she's reaching out for some attention."

Jackie and I shared a glance. Scott was so darned perceptive.

"Why don't you join us for dinner?" I asked. Raising my voice, I called to Roger, "Would you guys like to join us at the big house for dinner? You too, Devon and Luis. And I'll invite Ryan."

"That works for me," Roger said.

"I'm sorry," Luis said. "My mother is expecting her brother over to our house, and she wants all us kids there."

"Belinda already has a chicken in the crockpot," Devon said. "But I appreciate the offer."

Traffic into the café was quickly picking up, and I made a mental note to text Ryan as soon as there was a lull. The past twenty-four hours had certainly been crazy, even by Winter Garden's standards. I was hoping for a fun, peaceful evening, but I had a sneaking suspicion that we hadn't seen the last of the fall-out from last night's storm.

Chapter Two

"If only you could've been at the big house and seen how tickled Aunt Bess was at all the attention she was getting. I couldn't decide whether she looked more like a five-year-old at her birthday party or a queen holding court—I settled on a combination of the two.

"How sweet of all of you to put together this dinner in my honor." Patting the sofa cushion beside her, she said, "Scott, why don't you come sit by me? You know I enjoy hearing all your sister's fascinating stories, but you're my favorite."

I had no trouble imagining her saying the exact same thing to Scott's sister, Ivy. Ivy was the sheriff department's crime technician, and Aunt Bess loved to try to mine her for information she could put on her Pinterest boards. Aunt Bess's favorite social media platform was Pinterest. Her boards included *Crime Scenes*—the latest, *People I've Outlived*, *Things I'd Like to Eat but Won't Make*, and *Lord Have Mercy*.

Going back into the kitchen to see if Mom and Jackie needed any help reheating dinner, I said, "She's having a blast out there with all those handsome gentlemen."

In addition to Scott and Ryan, Mom's new beau and Winter Garden's only resident physician, Clark Bennett, was there. Roger hadn't arrived yet.

"She insisted on having Clark listen to her heart," Mom said.

"Her heart?" Jackie asked. "Has she been having chest pains?"

"No, and Clark told her she's more fit than most women half her age, but she still insisted he have his receptionist call her tomorrow and make an appointment."

Jackie's cell phone rang, and she fished it out of her back jeans pocket. "Hey, you. Where are you? We're hungry." Her voice went from chipper to solemn. "Oh, no. Do you want me to come to the hospital?"

Mom and I stilled.

Jackie finished her call and turned to us. "It's Devon. He was in a car accident. Roger was passing by and saw the accident. He stopped and called 9-1-1. He's waiting with Devon now."

"How is he?" I asked.

"Roger doesn't know. Devon keeps going in and out of consciousness."

Ryan stuck his head into the kitchen. "Hey, babe. Sorry, but I have to run. There's been an accident."

"We know," I told him. "It's Devon. He works with Roger. Roger's there waiting for the EMTs."

Ryan nodded. "I'll call you when I can."

Before Ryan could leave, Clark caught up to him. "Let me come with you. I might be able to help."

The two men had barely gotten out the door when Aunt Bess ambled into the kitchen on Scott's arm.

"They'll probably be a while, so we might as well eat," she said. "It's not that I'm insensitive—that Devon is a nice boy—but we're hungry, and there's nothing we can do for him at the moment." She sighed. "I hope he doesn't have any broken bones. That would be awful here at the holidays."

"She's right about them being gone for a while," Mom said. "Amy, would you and Jackie set the table please?"

"With pleasure," I said.

It didn't feel right sitting there eating dinner while Devon could be severely injured. We were all on pins and needles as we waited word on how he was doing—all except Aunt Bess, that is. To her way of thinking, he was probably fine, this was her celebratory dinner, and she wasn't going to waste it.

"Everything is so delicious," she said. "What's for dessert?"

"Lemon meringue pie," I said.

"Oh, good. That'll be nice and light after all the muffins and cookies I've had today. Why, not an hour after I posted online that I narrowly escaped death last night—"

"Aunt Bess!" Mom gaped at her.

"Well, I did! That roof could've fallen right in on top of me, and it's only by the grace of God that it didn't." She looked around the table at the rest of us. "And then, before you know it, people started sending me things. I got a lovely fruit basket from Sheriff Billings, a box of muffins from the fire department, another big assortment of fruit from the Senior Center—they keep wanting me to join up, but I'm not sure I want to spend that much time around all those *old* people, and I got cookies from the funeral home." She narrowed her eyes. "Looking back, I think those cookies might've been self-serving. They included a business card. Acted like I'd better be getting my affairs in order. Hmph. I said I'd escaped death, not invited it in and told it to have a seat and put its feet up."

None of us had a rebuttal to any of that—not even Scott—so we merely ate in silence.

Finally, Roger called Jackie. He asked her to put him on speaker and said he was bringing Clark back to pick up his car.

"We've kept plates warm for you," Jackie said.

"Thanks, but...um...I'm not up to eating," Roger said. "Devon died on route to the hospital."

"Oh, Roger." Tears pricked my eyes. "I'm so sorry."

"Me too," he said. "I don't know how long Ryan will be."

"Is there anything we can do?" Mom asked.

"Not tonight," Clark said. "I don't think I'm up for dinner either. I'm sorry."

"We understand," Jackie said. "See you when you get here." She ended the call.

I looked over to see Aunt Bess weeping softly and twisting her handkerchief in her hands. "I don't want to put that sweet boy on my *People I've Outlived* board."

Scott hugged her as he fought back tears of his own.

I took Ryan's meal to the police station. He was sitting at a computer typing up the accident report on Devon. He was the only person in the building, as far as I could tell.

"I'm sorry for how your evening turned out," I said from the doorway.

"Me, too." He swiveled in his chair and held his arms out to me. "Seeing you makes it better."

I went to him and we embraced.

"You never get used to finding someone like that...not being able to help," he said.

"I know." I didn't, of course, but I could imagine it would be terrible. What could I say that might help? "Are you hungry? I brought you some food."

"Thank you, sweetheart. You're awfully good to me." He took my hand and led me into the breakroom.

As I unpacked his food, I tried to come up with an innocuous subject of conversation so that maybe Ryan could eat without dwelling on the tragedy he'd just witnessed. "You know that felt gingerbread man ornament your mom made to go on my Christmas tree?"

"Yeah." He grabbed a soda from the refrigerator. "Want one?"

I shook my head. "I apparently hung the ornament too close to the bottom of the tree because Rory met me at the door with the poor thing in his mouth last night," I said. "He hadn't chewed on it, and in fact, he was being quite gentle with it. I hung it back on the tree, but I found it on the floor near his bed this morning."

Ryan chuckled. "Let him have it. There aren't any buttons on it he could swallow or anything."

"True. He's always preferred chew toys in the past. Every other stuffed animal I've given him, he's destroyed in seconds. I don't know why he's so enamored of this gingerbread man."

"He's a funny little guy, that's for sure."

"I can hardly wait for you to see him with it. He's so proud of it," I said. "But don't tell your mom."

"I'm calling her as soon as you leave." He arched a brow. "Unless you can change my mind."

"If that lemon meringue pie doesn't change your mind, I don't know what will."

"You've got me—" His cell phone rang, and he looked at the screen. "It's Ivy. I need to take this."

He returned to his desk to speak with Ivy privately and, I supposed, to take any necessary notes. In a town as small as Winter Garden, I couldn't imagine Ivy would be examining evidence on anything other than Devon's accident this evening. But why? She was a crime scene investigator, not an accident reconstructionist. Or maybe she was. I didn't know. I'm sure Ivy could do it. Not only was she a car enthusiast and a capable mechanic, I believed that woman could do anything she set her mind to.

"Is everything all right?" I asked Ryan when he returned to the breakroom.

He shook his head. "One of the EMTs said that when Devon was going in and out of consciousness, he said he couldn't stop. He said something along the lines of, 'The brakes weren't there.'"

"And you think maybe faulty brakes caused the accident?" I asked.

"I know it was the brakes—Ivy just confirmed it." He ran a hand down his face. "But they didn't go out for no reason—the brake lines were cut."

"Is it possible Devon ran over something and punctured the brake lines that way?" I didn't want to believe someone set out to sabotage Devon's vehicle.

Shaking his head, Ryan said, "Ivy reported there was no corrosion on the lines or any evidence that they were in poor condition. And the cuts were clean. She's convinced someone wanted Devon's brakes to fail."

"Someone wanted him to wreck and get hurt?" The thought was still absurd to me.

"He was going across Winter Garden mountain— that curvy road with the rocky cliff walls on one side and the drop-offs on the other. Whoever cut those brake lines most likely knew where Devon would be and that he couldn't survive a crash on that road."

"But—"

"Devon was murdered."

Chapter Three

Dilly and Walter were back at their usual table on Wednesday morning, but they were sad and subdued. I came out of the kitchen to give Dilly a hug.

"I just can't believe it," she said, her shoulders slumping. "Devon was such a sweet man. He didn't even charge me for coming out yesterday." Her thin lips spread into a half smile. "He said Roger would have his hide if he charged a sweetheart like me for simply resetting the breaker."

"That's what was wrong with the heat pump." Walter took off his tan newsboy cap and placed it on the table. "He told us that from now on when there's a power outage, we should turn off the heat pump until the power comes back on. That'll keep the mechanism from suffering any damage from a power surge when electricity is restored." He sighed. "He was sharp—that one. Knew his onions."

"I'd like to take a gift to Devon's wife," Dilly said. "Although I didn't know her, I'd like to take her a decorative stone I found that has a verse by Roy Lessin about the impact of one life on the world."

"I think that's a wonderful idea." I poured coffee into her cup. "Jackie and I are taking some food over to her later. Would you like to go with us?"

"I would."

"Roger is going too," Jackie said, "and I'm sure he'd be glad if you were there, Walter. He wouldn't want us to be all hens and only one rooster."

"Of course." Walter bobbed his head. "I'll be honored to join you."

Ryan came into the café, spoke to Dilly, Walter, and me, and then asked, "Jackie, may I have a word with you?" He avoided my eyes. "Privately?"

What was that about? Did he—like Devon—want to consult my cousin about a Christmas present he was considering buying? I thrilled to the thought before quickly dismissing it. Ryan's manner wasn't besotted boyfriend wanting to get advice on a piece of jewelry or a sweater. He was in police officer mode.

I dragged my eyes away from the patio where the two had gone to talk and turned my attention back to Dilly and Walter. "So, what are you two having for breakfast this morning?"

Walter ordered eggs Benedict, and Dilly chose biscuits and gravy. I went into the kitchen to get started on the hollandaise sauce.

When Jackie joined me in the kitchen a couple of minutes later, I asked, "Did Ryan want breakfast?"

"No." Mouth set in a firm line, she looked up at the order hanging above the grill and began to make the sausage gravy.

"What did he want?" I figured if it were—as I'd kinda hoped—a Christmas gift suggestion, she wouldn't be angry about it, so I didn't think it would hurt to ask.

"He was looking for Roger."

"Why? Did something happen at the police station?" Maybe the building had suffered some damage during the storm, and it was only being found now. Okay, I knew I was grasping at straws. But I didn't like the inevitable conclusion I was drawing.

And then Jackie said it: "Yeah, something happened. Roger became a suspect in Devon's murder."

I'd tried to reassure Jackie for the rest of the morning that Ryan didn't really consider Roger a suspect and that he was only doing his job, but it hadn't helped much. To be honest, I had to wonder about it myself. Ryan had barely spoken with me this morning, and then he'd taken off as soon as he'd asked Jackie about Roger. I felt uncomfortable with the entire situation, and I wanted to talk with Ryan about it as soon as possible. Or, at least, I thought I did.

When Homer came in at his usual time, he was greeted by Scott.

"Guru Guy! What's the good word today, dude?"

Smiling, Homer said, "The good word comes from John Muir. He said, 'Everybody needs beauty as well as bread, places to play in and pray in, where nature may heal and give strength to body and soul.'"

"Whoa." Scott nodded. "That's mega deep."

"I feel it when I come here to the café." Homer sat at the counter. "This place and you folks are my daily restorative."

"We feel the same way about you, Homer," I said.

"Who's John Muir?" Jackie asked.

"Dude, John Muir was an awesome writer—he wrote these wilderness discovery books that spoke about the majesty of national parks and how we all need to preserve our environment."

"That's right, Scott!" Homer winked at his friend. "I'm proud of you for knowing that, son."

"Me too." Scott poured Homer a cup of coffee. "That sausage biscuit is on the way, Guru Guy."

Homer Pickens came in every morning at around ten-thirty for a sausage biscuit. He was in his late sixties, had grown up without a father, and chose a new hero every day. Even before Scott began working at the café on a regular basis, he'd dubbed Homer Guru Guy. The title fit.

I noticed a man standing by the door. He was wearing a blue blazer and khaki pants, and he had his hands shoved into his pockets. "Good morning!" I called to him. "Welcome to the Down South Café. I'm Amy. Please have a seat wherever you'd like and let me know if there's anything I can help you with."

"You're the proprietor?" the man asked.

"I am." I stepped from behind the counter to speak with the newcomer.

"Amy, I'm Bryson Neal, your new town manager. My family and I moved to Winter Garden when I got the job, and I'm going around and introducing myself to the local merchants." He grinned. "And trying to drum up participants for the upcoming Christmas parade."

"That's fantastic," I said. "May I get you a cup of coffee?"

"Please." Mr. Neal walked over to the counter and sat beside Homer. He introduced himself, and Homer did likewise. "Might you be interested in making a float to advertise this lovely café in the Christmas parade, Amy?"

"I intended for the café to remain open during the parade," I said. "That way, patrons could drop in after the parade for hot chocolate, coffee, and cookies."

"I'll stay here and keep the café open, Amy-girl!" Scott said. "That way you can go out and advertise. I think making a float would be fun."

Thinking that sometimes Scott was too effusive for his own good, I said, "It would, but I don't have a farm wagon or anything like that. What could I possibly use for a float?"

"You have the perfect parade ride—your Bug!" He spread his arms like his suggestion was genius, but I didn't see how my little yellow Volkswagen Beetle was cool enough to be in a parade. I mean, it wasn't a Corvette convertible or something.

"While I find my little car adorable, I don't think all of Winter Garden will be delighted to stand on the street and watch me drive by in it," I said. "Although, if I tossed candy out the windows, it might be a draw for the kids."

"You're limiting yourself, girl! My philosophy is go big!" He looked at Homer. "Right, Guru Guy?"

"Elaborate," Homer said, refusing to commit himself to Scott's suggestion of going big until he knew what that meant.

"Picture this," Scott said. "We put a huge, decorated cake on the top of the car—a dummy cake on a luggage rack—and we make blue and yellow Down South Café signs for the doors. It'll be awesome!"

"It would be!"

I turned to see Luis, who was bussing a table, lending his support for Scott's idea with a wide smile on his face.

"That would be incredible," Luis said. "And Oscar and I could help run the café during the parade."

"It would be something people wouldn't soon forget," Mr. Neal added.

I contemplated decorating and putting a cake atop my Bug, and I couldn't suppress a giggle. "I'll see what I can come up with. How soon do you need an answer?"

"This coming Monday is the deadline for sign-ups." He looked around the dining room. "I'm counting on you gentlemen to continue helping me win her over. I believe a cake float would be excellent publicity for the café."

Decorating the cake and documenting the float's progress on social media might be fun too. It would add to the excitement of finishing the final product. On the other hand, it would be great to surprise Mom and Aunt Bess. Still, I needed to research how difficult it would be before committing to Mr. Neal that I'd take part in the parade.

"Mr. Muir said that 'in every walk with nature, one receives far more than he seeks.' That's how it is with me," Homer said. "I came in here seeking my usual sausage biscuit, and I received—I hope—the opportunity to help my friends make a float for the Christmas parade."

"Of course, you can help," I said. "If I decide to do it."

From the corner of my eye, I could see Scott giving Homer a thumbs up. I turned to give him what I hoped was a look of warning. It didn't work.

Scott laughed and announced, "Dudes, we're making a float!"

Chapter Four

I carried a chicken casserole in a lidded foil pan with a lasagna in another lidded pan on top of that, making my ability to see where I was going practically nil. Jackie couldn't help because she was carrying a tray of desserts. Thankfully, a man inside Belinda's home saw us coming and held the door open for us.

"Wow! You guys went all out!" he said.

I didn't know what to say to that given the circumstances under which we were there, so I ignored the comment and asked, "Could you please point us toward the kitchen?"

"Sure thing." He took the food from me and led Jackie and me through the living room and into the kitchen where Belinda was standing with her back to the sink conversing with an older woman.

"Thank you," I said, as he placed the food on the table.

Jackie followed suit, and Belinda said, "I see you two have met my charming brother Adam. But don't get your hopes up, ladies, he's happily married."

I squinted at Jackie in confusion. What a weird thing to say when we'd come here to pay our respects to Devon. Besides, Belinda knew both Jackie and I were already in relationships, didn't she? Maybe the poor woman had been simply trying to break the ice.

"Actually, we haven't met." I stuck out my hand. "Amy Flowers."

"Adam Tate." He gave me a brief but firm handshake before shaking Jackie's hand.

"Jackie Fonseca," she said. "I'm sorry for your loss."

Adam nodded. "Devon was a good man."

"Belinda, may I help you do anything?" Jackie asked.

"No, thanks." She walked out of the kitchen.

"Do you live here in Virginia?" I asked Adam.

"Nope. Florida born and raised. Never saw a reason to leave."

"You must've driven all night to get here," I said.

"Actually, I was already here." He gave me a lopsided smile. "I came up to Winter Garden to have an early Christmas celebration with Belinda and Devon. I wanted to stay with them for a few days before going back and spending the holiday with the rest of our family."

"Devon didn't mention that," Roger said, stepping into the kitchen in time to overhear Adam's words. "Had I known, I'd have given him a few days off." He sighed. "I wish I had."

"No need for *shouldas* and *wouldas*, my friend," Adam said. "If regrets were dollars, we'd all be millionaires. Am I right?" He held out his hand. "You must be Roger."

"I am."

"Adam is Belinda's brother," Jackie said, as Roger shook Adam's hand.

"Nice to meet you—sorry for the circumstances. Devon was a great guy."

Adam bobbed his head in agreement. "He sure was."

"You said you were here for a few days," I said to Adam. "Is your wife in the living room?"

"Uh...no. She's not with me. She's...um...she wasn't feeling well when I left Florida."

Gayle Leeson

"I'm sorry to hear that. Will she be here for the funeral?" I asked.

"No. I don't want her travelling alone...in her condition." He smiled. "She's pregnant."

"Congratulations."

Jackie and Roger echoed my sentiments.

Adam invited us to come into the living room, so we followed him. I was happy to see that Dilly and Walter had arrived. Dilly was presenting Belinda with the garden stone she'd brought, and Belinda was clasping it to her chest.

"Thank you," Belinda said. "It's beautiful."

"Your husband was a dear, sweet man," Dilly said. "I wish I could've known him longer."

I gazed around the room and wondered who else here knew that Devon had been murdered. Had the police even released that information to Belinda yet? If Adam knew, that might be another reason why he wouldn't want his pregnant wife here.

I looked at Adam, who was scanning the faces of everyone in the room. He met my eyes and smiled. Were we doing the same thing? Surely not. I couldn't imagine we shared the same reason for scrutinizing expressions. Or did we?

As we left the house, Jackie looked over her shoulder. Convinced only I could hear her, she said, "I don't know why Belinda was so standoffish to me."

I patted her back. "People deal with grief in different ways. I wouldn't take it personally."

"I can't help it. I'd have thought maybe she was angry with Roger because he'd sent Devon out to look at a job or something, but she was fine with him."

Jackie was right. Belinda had been warm and kind to everyone who'd come to pay their respects at the home, except for Jackie. Every time Jackie had attempted to speak with Belinda, the woman had cut her off and either walked away or spoken with someone else.

Recalling the remark Belinda had made about her brother, Adam, I asked, "Do you think she's jealous of you? Maybe Devon had given her a reason to think he admired you or something."

"That's ridiculous." She scoffed. "Roger admires a lot of women—you, for example—and I'm not jealous."

"True, but not all women are as secure and self-assured as you are." I grinned. "And, yeah, I am pretty wonderful. Have I ever told you how lucky you are to have me as a cousin?"

She stopped and gave me a glare that made me laugh out loud. Out of a sense of propriety, I stifled it quickly.

"By the way, you never did answer that question I asked you a few weeks ago," I said, recalling a conversation in which I'd offered for her to become my business partner.

"Yes, I'll marry you," she joked. "But I'm keeping Roger on the side."

"You know what I'm talking about."

"Yeah—the partnership. I don't know, Amy, the café is your thing. It was something you'd dreamed of for ages. I love working there with you, but I'm thinking of enrolling in some online classes and following a dream of my own."

"I think that's wonderful. I don't want to lose you—and I know the Down South Café patrons don't either—but we all want whatever will make you happy."

Smiling, she said, "Thanks."

"Any idea what type of classes you want to take?"

"I have until the spring to decide. Roger is trying to get me interested in architecture, but I'm leaning more toward accounting."

"I'm proud of you," I said.

"Ha, you just want cut-rate bookkeeping services."

I inclined my head. "That too."

After I got home and fed Rory and Princess Eloise, I went into the fancy room, and pulled out the few books I had on cake design. When Mom had lived here, the fancy room had been her bedroom. Roger had helped me renovate it into the cozy, totally girly room it was now.

Thumbing through the books, I knew I needed to have an enormous cake to go on top of the Bug, but I didn't want to give parade-goers the idea that I was in the business of making wedding cakes. That honor went to Daphne Martin—now Jacobs—in Brea Ridge. So, what could I make that was as big as a wedding cake but made to show patrons what they could expect if they visited the café? I grabbed a notebook and pen and turned to the books for inspiration.

The first thing I'd need was a sturdy cake board. Award-winning cake artist Rosemary Galpin of Luling, Texas, suggested using a half-inch thick plywood cake board pre-drilled for screws to attach to the carrier and a pipe flange in the center of the board to give added support. Reading the rest of the instructions on creating a cake board sturdy enough to carry my giant cake in the parade, I knew I'd need a professional. Dave Tucker was a wonderful woodworker—he'd participated in the farmers' market in the fall—and I was certain he could help me out. But I didn't have his number. I'd have to call his granddaughter, Amanda, who owned the fashion boutique Designs on You in Abingdon. I made a note to that effect in the margin of my notebook.

Rosemary also suggested six tiers of cake dummies, with the base being a sixteen-inch round and decreasing in two-inch increments up to a six-inch topper. I got out my laptop and searched for cake dummies. They were less expensive than I'd expected. I ordered the suggested six tiers and requested express shipping.

I'd searched through so many cakes that I was beginning to get a headache when I found the perfect inspiration—a coffee cup sitting upon a tier that appeared to be a chocolate cake atop a tier that resembled a table. I smiled and started to sketch. The bottom would be a round table, complete with a blue tablecloth with yellow stripes. Maybe I could add some flowers or flower petals strewn about.

The next tier would be all about breakfast. There would be eggs, pancakes, toast, bacon, muffins, and scones. Then would come lunch—chicken legs, hot dogs, cheeseburgers, salads, and sandwiches. The fourth tier would feature slices of pie and cake, cookies, brownies, and desserts such as ice cream and parfaits. Like the cake which inspired me, I decided to make the fifth tier a cake—but not a chocolate cake, a Christmas cake. And the final cake would be a cup of coffee.

My drawing abilities left a lot to be desired, but I was excited about the cake. This was going to be so much fun! Also, a ton of work. But fun! I hoped.

I called Bryson Neal and told him that Down South Café would have a float in the parade.

Chapter Five

Scott, Jackie, and Luis already knew by the time Homer arrived on Thursday morning that I'd agreed to make a float for the Winter Garden Christmas Parade. I'd instructed them—Scott, mainly—to let me be the one to tell Homer. Luckily, the café wasn't terribly busy when he arrived, and I had a few minutes to visit with him.

"Good morning, Homer," I said. "Who's your hero today?"

He told me it was the novelist Richard Bach. "Did you know it was Mr. Bach who said, 'What the caterpillar calls the end of the world, the Master calls the butterfly'?"

"I didn't know that." I smiled. "But I've always loved that quote."

"Me too." He glanced at his watch.

Knowing he was getting antsy about sticking to his strict self-imposed schedule, I said, "Jackie is at the grill frying your sausage patty. I have news about the float."

Eyes widening, he grinned. "We're gonna do it. We're making a float."

"That's right." I got out my cake sketch and explained how I wanted to construct it. "I've already ordered the cake dummies, and they should be here by Saturday."

Homer pointed to my note in the margin. "Pardon me if I'm out of line, but I notice here you've made a note to call Amanda Tucker to get her grandfather's phone number. Have you done that yet?"

"Not yet. I haven't had time."

"I have Dave's number at home," he said. "I'll call you back with it later this afternoon."

"Thank you, Homer. I appreciate that."

"May I ask why you're calling Dave?"

I explained about the cake board.

Homer nodded. "Yeah, if anybody can help with that, it's Dave. But, you know, I'll be happy to help to...you know...in whatever way I can."

"Well, if those cake dummies come in on Saturday like they're supposed to, I'm thinking of getting started on the float Sunday after lunch." I frowned. "I've never undertaken something this huge before, and I'm afraid I'll fall flat on my face. I need plenty of time to factor my mistakes into getting the project done on time."

"Mr. Bach once said there are no mistakes. 'The events we bring upon ourselves, no matter how unpleasant, are necessary in order to learn what we need to learn; whatever steps we take, they're necessary to reach the places we've chosen to go.' You'll be fine."

I nodded slightly. *Sorry, Homer, but I prefer not to think about bringing unpleasant events upon myself at the moment.* "I'll go see how Jackie is doing with that biscuit."

Roger came in with two of his crew, and the men ordered brunch. By then, I was back at the grill, and Jackie took their orders. When she brought the tickets to the window, she mentioned that one of the young men with Roger was Aaron, who used to bus tables for us. I went to the window and waved.

"Hey, Amy!" He gave me a wide grin. "Merry Christmas!"

"Don't crowd the season. We still have nearly three weeks. But Merry Christmas to you too."

Homer decided this would be a perfect time to interject a Richard Bach quote. "I've heard 'every gift from a friend is a wish for your happiness.' Isn't that nice?"

"It is," Roger said. "I like that, Homer. How're you doing, buddy?"

Leaving the men to their chat, I focused on preparing their pancakes and cheeseburgers. People had varying tastes when the clock neared eleven. Some still wanted breakfast while others were ready for lunch.

I'd just plated their meals when I heard Scott say, "Hey, dude! You here to eat, or are you just visiting the boss?"

Guessing Scott was addressing Ryan, I put the plates on a tray and took them out to Roger and his crew myself. I was right—Ryan was standing there next to Roger's table looking handsome as always in his uniform.

Giving my sweetheart a broad smile, I said, "Hi, there! Our special today is barbecue chicken if you're interested."

"I'd love to stay, but I'm here in an official capacity," he said. "Roger, I'll see you in about half an hour then?"

Roger nodded. "I'll be there."

Ryan kissed my cheek and told me he'd see me later.

"What was that about?" Jackie asked.

I had an idea, of course, but I thought it best to let Roger answer.

"Ryan stopped by because he saw my truck here," Roger said. "He wants me to come to the police station after I eat."

"Why?" Jackie looked from Roger to me and then back to Roger.

I hadn't felt at liberty to tell anyone else that Devon's wreck hadn't been an accident since Ryan had gotten the information while I was at the station, and I'd felt he had told me in confidence. I'd never do anything to compromise an investigation, and I knew my friends wouldn't want that either.

Roger gave Jackie a little shrug and put butter and syrup on his pancakes. "Guys, go on over to the Flowers house and continue working on the roof after we eat. I'll be there as soon as I can."

"I don't understand," Jackie said. "What's this about?"

"I'm guessing it has something to do with Devon," Roger said.

A couple I'd never seen before walked into the café. I welcomed them, told them about our special of the day, and then went back to the kitchen.

Jackie followed me. "What's going on?"

"You know as much as I do." That wasn't entirely true, but I didn't know for certain that Ryan wanted to speak with Roger about Devon's accident. Maybe someone filed a complaint against one of Roger's workers for harassment or shoddy workmanship or something. Unlikely, but possible.

"I don't believe that," Jackie said. "You know something."

"I know whatever is going on, Ryan asked Roger to come to the station on official business under orders of Sheriff Billings. It's nothing personal."

"Really? It feels personal to me." She glanced toward the dining room. "That could explain why Belinda was being hateful to me last night. She knew she was getting ready to file a wrongful death suit or something against Roger since Devon was on the clock at the time of the crash, and she felt guilty about it because she knows it wasn't Roger's fault."

"Jackie, if Belinda wanted to file a wrongful death suit, she'd have to go to an attorney, not the police.

And even if she did—which I doubt—the ball wouldn't be rolling this quickly."

Blowing out a breath, she said, "I know. You're right. I'm just worried, that's all."

"Everything will be fine. We all know—Ryan included—that Roger would never do anything to hurt anyone."

"Wait. You think someone messed with Devon's truck?" She took hold of my arm. "Do the police think someone caused the crash that killed him?"

Scott came up to the window. "Two chef salads, one without cucumber and onions."

"Thanks." Waiting until Scott walked away, I added, "I'm speculating—the same as you. All I meant was that if anybody is suspected of any kind of foul play, we know Roger is innocent. Okay?"

She nodded, turned, and left the kitchen.

Homer stood and called into the kitchen, "See you later, Amy! Remember, 'the simplest things are often the truest.' Have a wonderful day!"

"Take care, Homer!" I smiled as I heard the rest of the dining room—with the exception of the newcomers—bidding farewell to one of our favorite regulars. Although I didn't let on, I was as nervous as Jackie was about Roger's meeting at the police station.

Chapter Six

After work, I took dinner to Mom and Aunt Bess. Before going inside, I tried to check the progress on the roof. I thought it looked fine, but I couldn't tell how much still needed to be done. Roger's crew had called it a day. I wondered how his interview at the police station had gone.

Mom saw me coming and held open the kitchen door for me. "Something sure does smell good."

"Barbecue chicken." I carried the pan into the house and placed it on the counter. After turning the oven on, I sat down at the table. "Where's Aunt Bess?"

"In the living room." Mom sat across from me. "Why? What's wrong?"

"Probably nothing, but Ryan came in today and asked Roger to come to the police station for an interview," I said.

"An interview?" Aunt Bess asked from the doorway. "Is Roger joining the police force? He'd better not before he gets our roof fixed!" She came on into the kitchen and joined us at the table.

"It wasn't that kind of an interview." I got up from the table and poured myself a glass of water. "The police said Devon's accident was caused because someone cut his brake lines."

Aunt Bess gasped. "Devon was *murdered*? And they think Roger did it?" She shook her head. "I don't believe that for an instant. Roger's a good boy—I've known him practically all his life."

"I agree," Mom said. "Maybe they merely wanted to ask Roger some questions about who might've had it in for Devon."

After asking if anyone else wanted a glass of water—no one did—I sat back down. "I can't imagine Ryan believes Roger cut Devon's brake lines either. He's simply doing his job. But Jackie certainly is upset about it."

Aunt Bess flicked her wrist. "She'll be all right. She knows that we have to treat everybody as a suspect until we discover who all had the means, motive, and opportunity to do the deed." She nodded so emphatically it set her tight curls to jiggling. "Then we can narrow down our suspect pool and fish out the true culprit."

I glanced over to see Mom pinching the bridge of her nose, and I almost laughed out loud. So what if Aunt Bess wanted to count herself among the great detectives? I thought it was fun. But, then again, I didn't have to live with her.

"Didn't that boy come here from somewhere else?" Aunt Bess asked.

"Yes," I said. "He came here from Florida. I think he used to run a fishing boat charter."

"How'd he wind up here in Winter Garden?" Mom asked.

"I recall Roger saying Devon inherited a piece of property when his aunt died and that he had fond memories of coming to Winter Garden to visit her and her family during the summers." I shrugged slightly. "I guess he thought it would be a good place to live."

"But why give up his business in Florida unless it was in the dumps?" Aunt Bess asked.

Admitting she had an excellent point, I said, "Maybe it wasn't his business. Some people can be terrible to work for." I knew that from experience. The woman who'd owned the café before me had been an atrocious boss. "It could be Devon was looking for a way out, and his aunt's leaving him some property was the opportunity he'd been waiting for."

"Does he have family here?" Mom asked. "If he has cousins, I wonder how they felt about his benefiting from their mother's death?"

"That's a good point." I smiled. "You two really do make good detectives—Sherlock and Watson."

"I prefer to think of us as Charlie's angels." Aunt Bess patted her curls. "That way, you're included too. But, of course, I'm the hot one."

"They were all hot," Mom said, through gritted teeth.

"That's right." Aunt Bess gave Mom's hand a condescending pat. Then she looked at me. "Devon's been here—what—six or seven months?"

"I believe so," I said.

"Angry cousins could be the very boogers that killed that boy." The oven clicked and the preheat light went off. Aunt Bess nodded toward the appliance. "Shouldn't somebody be putting that chicken in to heat up?"

Ryan came over after work, and we watched a Christmas movie on television. During a commercial break, I wondered how to broach the subject of Roger being a suspect in Devon's murder.

"Mom, Aunt Bess, and I were talking about Devon earlier today." That seemed like an adequate start. "We heard something about how he left Florida because his aunt left him some property here in Winter Garden." I looked at him from the corners of my eyes while I fidgeted with the fringe on a blanket I had beside me on the sofa. "Aunt Bess seemed to think some angry cousins might be responsible for Devon's death."

"Good point." Ryan gently bopped Rory's nose with the gingerbread man the dog had presented to him. "Right, Rory? Yes, it is! Yes, that's right!" He tossed the toy, and Rory scampered after it.

"Then you are looking at the cousins," I said.

He gave me a look that reminded me of the department's—and his—policy on not discussing active cases, especially ones involving my friends.

"I'm just guessing there are a lot of suspects in a case like this." I accidentally pulled a thread out of the fringe and tucked it inside the folds of the blanket. "Right?"

Rory bounded back with the gingerbread man. Ryan took it and tossed it again.

"Do we really want to talk about this?" he asked.

"No." I nestled against his side. "I just—Roger isn't really a suspect...is he?"

"Oh, look," he said. "The movie's back on."

That night, I had the strangest dream. Ryan and I were in a Christmas movie. At first, I thought it was a romantic comedy. I was the wide-eyed girl who'd returned to her hometown to follow her dream of opening a café. He was the handsome lawman who'd never left. While I was trying to decide whether he was trying to teach me the meaning of Christmas or the other way around, Rory came running into the scene.

That's when I realized the "scene" was an outdoor Christmas tree lighting with all of Winter Garden gathered around: There was Dilly. She was standing beside Walter and was holding her raccoon. The raccoon was wearing a red crocheted scarf and hat, and the hat had a pompom on the top. I thought that was the cutest thing. I waved, and the raccoon waved back. In the dream, I wasn't even surprised.

There was Homer. His hero of the day was Santa Claus, and he was spouting off quotes like, "As the jolly one would say, 'Ho, ho, ho!" and "Merry Christmas to all, and to all, a good night." Scott was dressed as an elf, and at Homer's words of—of what? merriment? good cheer?—Scott would encourage him with cries of, "Way to go, Jolly Dude!" and "Tell it like it is, Goodwill Guru!"

Aunt Bess and Mom were off to the side where they could observe everything. It appeared they were at the ceremony to serve and protect, although I knew that was Ryan's job. Maybe he was off duty? Anyway, Mom and Aunt Bess stood back to back, and each held some sort of pistol—barrel up—in front of her face. They wore black jumpsuits and looked fantastic. The dream had shaped them into angels the likes of which Charlie would have been proud.

Ryan winked at me and squeezed my hand before stooping down to address Rory. "What's the matter, buddy? Are you spooked by the crowd?"

But, no, it wasn't the crowd that had Rory in a fright. It was the felt gingerbread man Ryan's mom had made for my Christmas tree. It had grown to a height of a hundred feet tall, dwarfing the Christmas

tree at the center of the tree lighting ceremony by at
least forty feet! That was the moment that I realized
I wasn't starring in a romantic comedy. This movie
was a horror film!

It also dawned on me that I hadn't picked Roger
and Jackie out of the crowd yet. I scanned the faces
near me. None of them were Roger and Jackie. I began to run. Even though a giant gingerbread man
was heading down the sidewalk, it appeared that I
was the only person aware of it. I stopped amid clus-
ters of people to determine whether Roger and Jackie were among them. Finally, I saw them. They were
right in the path of the gingerbread man! I ran, but I
wasn't fast enough. The gingerbread man crushed
Roger beneath one icing-laced foot.

I awoke with a start. Rather than looking for
Roger and Jackie, I should have been finding a way
to stop the gingerbread man.

Chapter Seven

Upon arriving at the café Friday morning, I was surprised to find that Jackie was already there. I got out of my car and hurried inside. The coffee pots had been prepared, but I didn't see Jackie in the dining room.

I went through to the kitchen where I found her shredding lettuce. "Is everything all right?"

She shook her head. "No. I'm worried about this whole thing with Devon."

"Oh, come on." I tied on an apron. "No one is seriously considering Roger as a suspect. Everybody knows he's a great guy."

"The sheriff apparently doesn't." She put down the head of lettuce she'd been holding and turned to look at me. "When he and Ryan talked with Roger yesterday, they asked him about an argument he had with Devon a few days ago."

I frowned. "Devon and Roger argued? About what?"

"Roger learned that Devon was trying to get cheaper versions of name-brand appliances for a home the crew is currently renovating."

"Why would Devon do that?" I asked. "The money for the appliances wasn't coming out of his pocket."

"No, but if it took less money to pay for the appliances than what he was given, then he could keep the difference." Jackie resumed shredding the lettuce. "Roger's crew knows he doesn't cut corners, and he was furious with Devon. I believe he was also hurt that Devon would go behind his back like that."

"I'm surprised Roger didn't fire Devon on the spot." I took the sausage from the refrigerator and began forming it into patties.

"He would have had it not been so close to Christmas," she said. "Plus, he liked Devon. He wanted to give him a second chance. And, yeah, the deal caused Roger a lot of headaches—he had to cancel the order for the cheaper appliances, go buy the right ones—but it was certainly nothing he'd kill a man over. Fire, yes? Kill, never. And he couldn't even pull the trigger on firing Devon."

"Surely Sheriff Billings understands that. Everyone gets angry—and it sounds as if Roger had an excellent reason for doing so."

"True. But to him—and Ryan—it looks like Roger was the one with the means, motive, and opportunity."

"That's ridiculous. They know it, and they won't stop looking for Devon's real killer."

I heard the door open, peeped through the window into the dining room, and then went to greet Dilly and Walter. I said a silent prayer that the sheriff would find Devon's murderer soon.

Fridays were typically busy at the café, and today had been no exception. It was getting close to quitting time when Devon's wife, Belinda, walked in. She gazed around the dining room, in which only Mr. Poston and his son lingered over hot dogs and sodas.

"Welcome to the Down South Café," Scott said brightly. "Would you like to hear today's special, or is there something in particular you'd like to try?"

"I'm here to speak with Jackie Fonseca more than anything," Belinda said.

"Sure." Jackie walked out of the kitchen. "Would you care for some coffee or a glass of water?"

"A glass of water would be nice. Thank you." Belinda sat at the counter. "Did Devon eat here often?"

Not knowing whether I'd need to use the grill again before closing up for the day, I helped Luis clean the tables. Also, I was curious as to what Belinda wanted to speak with Jackie about—especially since the woman had been so unfriendly to my cousin on Wednesday evening. Jackie always had my back, and I wanted to be there to defend her if Belinda got rude.

"Sometimes Roger and his crew—if any of them are working in Winter Garden—stop in for lunch but not that often," Jackie said. "They take too many jobs out of town."

"That's good," Scott chimed in. "Winter Garden is so small, a person could blink and drive right past it. If Roger did all his business here, he wouldn't have much to do."

"That's the truth!" Mr. Poston chuckled. "Thank goodness people like to read and that they come to my bookshop from all over the region or else I'd have gone belly up years ago."

"Once in a while if the café has too many leftovers at the end of the day, I'll take some home and Roger will share them with his workers the next day," Jackie said. "It's mainly cookies or brownies. But every so often, we have chicken salad or tuna salad, and I make sandwiches for the crew."

"That's nice," Belinda said, her voice a bit on the icy side. "How well did you know Devon?"

"About as well as I know anyone in Roger's crew." Jackie glanced over at me.

I pretended to studiously wipe off the table in front of me, although if I wasn't careful, I was going to rub the finish off the top.

Mr. Poston and his son paid and left the restaurant.

Scott sidled next to me. "Want me to clean the grill? I don't think this woman is going to order anything."

"Would you please?" I smiled, guessing he knew I wanted to eavesdrop.

He winked. "I think that table's good now. Might want to move on to another one."

I playfully swatted at him with my towel.

Jackie came around the counter and sat on a stool beside Belinda. "There's something I need to confess to you."

Belinda stiffened. "All right. Let's have it then."

"I probably shouldn't be telling you this, but I think Devon would want you to know. He loved you very much."

"Right. That's what you shouldn't be telling me?" Belinda asked.

"No. What I shouldn't be telling you is that Devon and I had planned to meet tomorrow," Jackie said.

I raised my head at Belinda's sharp intake of breath.

Jackie hurried on. "We were going to get your Christmas present. It was supposed to be Devon's day off, but he planned to tell you that Roger needed him to work."

Belinda gulped her water. "M-may I have more please?"

"Of course," Jackie said.

"I'll get it." I left my cleaning supplies on the table and went to refill Belinda's water glass.

"We'd been working on our plan for weeks," Jackie said. "He wanted to get you something special, and given his hectic work schedule, he had me trying to track it down."

"Track what down?" Belinda asked. "This is the first I'm hearing of any of this."

"Well, that was the point—to surprise you." Jackie smiled. "He wanted to get you a necklace, but it had to be the perfect necklace—one like the necklace you said your grandmother always wore. He said you'd described it so often—"

At that point, Belinda gave a strangled sob, slid off the stool, and raced out the door.

Jackie stood and hurried after her. "Belinda, wait!"

Either Belinda hadn't heard Jackie, or she'd chosen to ignore her because she got into her car and drove away.

Turning to us in bewilderment, Jackie asked, "Did I handle that poorly? Should I not have told her about the necklace?" Her voice faltered. "I thought she should know."

"Of course, she should have." I went over and patted Jackie's shoulder. "She was just overcome with emotion, that's all."

I hoped I was right. It was a weird reaction for Belinda to simply get up and flee the café without another word.

"Given the questions she was asking, I think that chick thought maybe you and her husband were having a fling," Scott said, coming from the kitchen into the dining room.

"What?" Jackie asked.

"Sure. She wanted to know how often her man came in here, how well you knew him..." He spread his hands. "Jealous woman 101."

"He's right," Luis said. "Maybe that's why she ran away like she did. She was ashamed of thinking badly of you. And of him, for that matter."

My gaze locked onto Jackie's. Scott's words did make sense. And Belinda's jealousy would certainly account for her behavior on Wednesday evening.

Chapter Eight

After work, I went home to shower and change and to feed the pets. Then I drove to the hobby shop to buy fondant and decorator icing for my giant cake. I wanted to be ready to begin work as soon as the cake dummies arrived. On the way there, I used Bluetooth to call Sarah. She'd been one of my best friends since elementary school.

"Hi, there!" Sarah answered brightly. "What are you up to?"

"Would you believe me if I said I'm getting ready to make a giant cake to put on top of my car and drive through town in the Christmas parade?"

She laughed. "You, yes. Anyone else? I'd have trouble believing it."

"Are you free for dinner?" I asked. "Ryan has to work tonight."

"I'd love to have dinner with you. John is having to stay at school all weekend to finish up a project that's due on Monday."

Sarah's boyfriend attended law school in Grundy, which was a little over an hour and a half away from Winter Garden.

"When does his winter break start?" I hoped he'd be able to come home soon.

"His classes wind up this coming Thursday, so he'll be home in a week," she said. "I'll have to get used to having him around again. He'll be home for three weeks."

"Well, the parade is next Saturday, so it's good to know where I can find another strong pair of arms should I need any extra help getting this cake up on-to the roof." I knew the cake wouldn't be *that* heavy and that Scott and Luis could place it onto the roof just fine, but I exaggerated to get a laugh out of Sa-rah. It worked.

"We wouldn't miss that parade now for the world. We'd been planning to skip it but wait until I tell John about your giant cake!" After she stopped giggling, she asked, "Where do you want to have dinner?"

"I'm on my way to the hobby shop, so would you like to meet somewhere in Bristol or Abingdon?" I asked. "Or I can come back to Winter Garden and pick you up."

"No, let's meet in Bristol. Maybe we can get some shopping in before we head back home."

"Sounds good," I said. We decided on a restaurant, and I ended the call as I pulled into the parking lot of the craft store.

I got some pretty strange looks as I made my way to the checkout counter a short while later with my cart filled with two twenty-pound tubs of white fondant and fifteen bottles of gel food coloring in assorted colors. I also had a few tools and molds I thought might come in handy.

Later, at the restaurant, I told Sarah how I wished I'd been able to think of something clever to say to the cashier.

"Something like, 'These elementary school parties are getting out of control—am I right?' Nah, that falls flat." I screwed up my face. "I guess I was better off keeping my mouth shut."

"How about..." She tapped her index finger on her chin, her coral fingernail polish providing a lovely

Gayle Leeson

contrast to her caramel-colored skin. Finally, she grinned. "Is it just me, or is the leaving cookies for Santa thing getting way too competitive lately?"

"That's a good one!" My laughter was interrupted by two men coming over to our table. One of them looked vaguely familiar, but I couldn't place him. "May I help you?"

"Yeah—sorry," said the man closest to me. "I'm Adam, Devon Carpenter's brother-in-law. We met at their house the other night?"

"Of course." I introduced Adam to Sarah.

"I'm sorry for your loss," she said.

"Thank you," Adam said, turning to the man at his side. "This is Chris. He's one of Devon's cousins. We saw you here and just wanted to say hello and to thank you for the food you brought to Belinda's. That was awfully nice of you."

"And the food was delicious," Chris said.

"How is Belinda?" I asked. "She was in the café earlier today, and she ran away as Jackie was telling her that she and Devon were planning to shop for her Christmas present tomorrow."

Adam nodded. "She told us about that—said Devon and your cousin had been trying to find her a necklace like our grandma used to wear."

{ 74 }

"Right. I'm glad she got home okay. We were concerned about her."

"She's grieving, that's all." Adam shrugged. "This ordeal has broken her heart."

"Even more now that she's found out about the necklace," Chris said. He ignored the dirty look Adam cast his way and continued, "I guess because it showed her how much he cared about her and that it would've been something to remember him by."

I looked across the table at Sarah and found that she appeared to be as confused as I felt. What were these guys—these strangers—doing standing at our table talking about someone I barely knew and whom Sarah didn't know at all?

"Did Devon talk much to you about Florida?" Adam asked.

"No. I'm afraid I didn't know Devon all that well," I said. "We'd only spoken briefly on the few occasions he'd been into the café."

"Right. I should ask Jackie," he said. "She might know if he'd discussed wanting to return."

"Why do you ask?" I found it bizarre that he would even care at this point whether Devon had ever wanted to go back to Florida. Unless... "Are you hoping Belinda will return home with you?"

"Uh, yeah. That'd be good...you know...for her to be with her family now that Devon's gone."

I saw our waiter approaching with our food and nodded to him. Adam turned to see what was going on and moved out of the waiter's way.

"I'll let you two fine ladies enjoy your meal," he said. "Have a good one."

"You too," I said.

The waiter placed our food in front of us and asked if we needed anything further. When we declined, he said he'd be back to check on us later.

When he was out of earshot, I asked, "Was that encounter with Adam and—what was his name—Chris? —weird, or was it just me?"

"Oh, it was weird all right." Sarah poured steak sauce onto the side of her plate. "They didn't seem terribly broken up about Devon's death. One acted like Devon's death would've meant more to his wife had she gotten the necklace he'd enlisted Jackie's help in finding, and the other was only interested in learning if Devon wanted to move back to Florida."

"Maybe Devon and his brother-in-law didn't get along and that now that Devon's dead, Adam wants his sister to move back home," I said. "That Chris guy gave me the impression that Devon and Belinda hadn't been getting along. Why else would he have said what he did about Belinda being even more heartbroken now that she's found out about the necklace?"

"I found that strange too," Sarah said, cutting into her steak. "Didn't Adam say Chris was Devon's cousin?"

"Yeah, he did. And Jackie told me Devon moved here because Devon's aunt left him some property." My growling stomach prompted me to stop talking and start eating. But I couldn't resist adding, "You know, inheritances have long been sources of family rifts."

"You don't have to tell me—I work in a law office."

Sarah was the administrative assistant to Billy Hancock, Winter Garden's one and only resident attorney.

I swallowed the bite of Parmesan crusted chicken I'd taken and wiped my mouth on my napkin. "You know, Belinda was acting kind of suspicious of Jackie when she was in the café today. Scott intimated that Belinda had probably thought something was going on between Devon and Jackie."

"Dang! I hope she didn't cut Devon's brake lines thinking he was cheating on her with Jackie!" Sarah grinned to soften her words, but her smile quickly faded. "Look slightly to your left, but don't be conspicuous."

I gave a fake laugh and turned my head. Devon's cousin, Chris, was sitting across the room staring at us. His expression was dark and calculating. It gave me chills.

Chapter Nine

On Saturday morning, Ryan brought his parents in for breakfast. I overheard Jackie ask Scott if he would wait on them.

"Sure thing!" Scott said, as he grabbed three menus and hurried over to their table.

"Gee," I said quietly, "you really are upset with Ryan."

"Actually, I thought that if Scott waited on them, I could man the grill so you could go say hello."

"Oh...right. Sorry."

She gave me a sheepish half-smile. "That, and I'm avoiding Ryan."

Ryan's dad, David, was a sweetheart. He smiled, rose, and hugged me when I approached the table. "How're you doing, Amy? Ready for Christmas?"

In appearance and personality alike, David looked like an older version of Ryan. Both men had the same dark brown hair and eyes—although David had a smattering of gray in his hair now—and both were warm and generous. A lovely redhead, Ryan's mom, Michelle, could be a bit cold, at least where I was concerned.

"Not quite. I think I might've bitten off more than I can chew," I said. "Did Ryan tell you about the cake I'm making for the parade?"

I included Michelle in my question, and she responded with a tight smile. She hadn't risen to give me a hug, and I'd have been shocked if she had.

"Are you talking about the gigantic fake cake you're going to make for the parade?" David asked.

"Well, I don't know that I'd call it *gigantic*," I said.

"It'll have to be pretty big to be seen in that parade." David grinned. "Ryan tells us you're going to put it on top of your car."

"Yep. On a luggage rack." I joined in David's laughter as he sat back down and took a sip of his coffee.

"I've decorated a few cakes in my day," Michelle said. "Let me know if you'd like any help."

"I'd love some," I said. "The cake dummies are scheduled to arrive today, and I plan on getting started here at the café tomorrow after lunch."

Michelle's face froze. I was guessing she wished she hadn't said anything.

"That'd be great, hon," David said. "You and Amy can work on the cake, and Ryan and I can hang out and watch the football game at home."

"All right," Michelle said. "Is there anything you'd like me to bring?"

"I believe I have everything we'll need to get started, and that's my main goal for tomorrow."

Scott joined us then. "I heard you talking about working on the cake tomorrow. Can I get in on that?"

"Of course." I smiled. "I'll take all the help I can get."

"Radical! This is gonna be awesome, dudes." He winked at Michelle. She looked as if she'd caught a whiff of something foul.

"I'll get out of your hair so Scott can take your orders," I said. "See you in a bit."

As I was walking away from Ryan's table, Adam and Chris ambled in. I felt my face tighten with sur-

Gayle Leeson

prise before I recovered enough to welcome the pair to the café.

Adam merely nodded at my greeting, and Chris gave me one of those inscrutable looks he'd given me the evening before when Sarah and I had been at dinner. They sat at the counter.

"Coffee?" I asked.

"Please," Adam said.

Chris shook his head. "Never touch the stuff. You got soft drinks?"

"Sure." After providing their options, Adam went with the dark roast coffee, and Chris chose cola. I poured their drinks and handed them menus. "Take a look and let me know what appeals to you."

"Thanks." Adam sipped the coffee. "That's good. It's cold out there."

"Cold?" I laughed. "It's warm right now. Sometimes I don't even have to wear a coat outside yet."

"It's cold here when you've recently come from Florida," he said. "There, it's balmy all the time."

"I hadn't considered that. How's Belinda this morning?"

Shaking his head, he sighed. "Not great. We made Devon's funeral arrangements this morning. She was lying down when I left."

"If there's anything I can do—" I let the hollow suggestion hang in the air. "As you mentioned last night, it would probably be nice for Belinda to go back to Florida where she can be around her family and friends."

"I think so." Adam took another sip of his coffee and then picked up his menu. "Nothing here for her anymore but sad memories, right?"

"I imagine so. Maybe she could sell their home and have enough to make a fresh start somewhere." I glanced at Chris. "Don't you think?"

Chris shrugged. "I don't know why not. I don't want her place. None of the rest of the family does either."

"I heard that Devon's aunt left him the property," I said. "Was that aunt your mom?"

"Yeah, why?"

"No reason...but that's a generous bequest for an aunt to make to her nephew. Some families would have resented him getting that big of an inheritance." I smiled. "Your family must be really big-hearted."

"Sure, we loved Devon. None of us cared that Mom left him that crummy little summerhouse that no one else wanted." He scoffed. "We got the good stuff."

"I'm sorry," I said. "I didn't mean to offend you. It's just that my friend works in a law office, and she's told me horror stories about how greedy some people can be toward their family members."

"Yeah, well, we're not like that," Chris said.

"Did Devon ever talk about his boat business while he was in here?" Adam asked. "I used to wonder if he missed it. Always thought he might come back to it, you know?"

"I bet he would have after spending a winter here, especially a winter working construction." Chris nudged Adam with his elbow. "You Florida boys have thin blood."

"Right—but you didn't give Amy a chance to answer my question. Did Devon ever mention it?"

"Not to me." I nearly let out a breath of relief when Homer entered the café. "Good morning, Homer. Who's your hero today?"

"Hello, Amy. Gentlemen." He took his usual seat which was two seats down from the one currently occupied by Adam. "My hero of the day is Alexander Pope, the English poet, who said, 'No one should be ashamed to admit he is wrong, which is but saying, in other words, that he is wiser today than he was yesterday.'"

"Guru Guy!" Scott called. "Good to see, man!"

"And you as well, Scott."

"I'll have your sausage biscuit out in just a minute," I told Homer. To Adam and Chris, I added, "Let me know when you're ready to order."

"Will do," Adam said, turning toward Homer. "Do you come here every day?"

"Yes, sir, I do," Homer said.

"Did you know Devon Carpenter?"

I wanted to linger to see what Adam wanted with Homer, but I knew Homer was ready for his biscuit. I hurried into the kitchen and asked Jackie to get the biscuit ready. "I'll be back as quickly as I can."

Pouring Homer a cup of coffee, I overheard him say, "He once mentioned sailing to the Bahamas. My hero of the day was the musician Lenny Kravitz, who has a home in the Bahamas. Devon said he'd traveled there and had hoped to meet Mr. Kravitz but that it wasn't in the cards for him."

Adam nodded slowly. "I remember hearing him talk about that now. Too bad he never got to meet the guy. What else did Devon say about the Bahamas?"

"Only that I should visit there," Homer said. "Although I'm a creature of habit and not one prone to wander from home, I promised Devon that should I ever be bitten by the travel bug, I'd add the islands to my itinerary."

"Did he tell you where you might want to go or give you a list of must-sees?" Adam asked.

"No." Homer chuckled. "He knew I wasn't likely to ever travel, and he never struck me—on the few occasions we spoke—as a man who dwelt overmuch on the past, including the places he'd been. He seemed to realize—like Alexander Pope—that fish tales are like this: 'And all who told it added something new, and all who heard it, made enlargements too.'"

"Huh?" Chris asked, wrinkling his brow.

"I suppose I'm trying to say that Devon seemed to be a man who lived in the moment," Homer said.

"We should all be blessed with that mentality," Adam said.

"That's the truth," Scott said. "I'm sure that's the credo Homer lives by too. Correct me if I'm wrong, Guru Guy."

"You're not wrong," Homer said.

At the end of the workday, Jackie and I divvied up the desserts. We took the remainder of the pecan pie to serve at Sunday lunch—each Sunday we meet at the big house and make lunch for Mom and Aunt Bess—and she took some snickerdoodles. Luis took cupcakes and brownies, Scott took chocolate chip and sugar cookies, and I took the remaining oatmeal cookies. I thought I could serve the cookies if we started running low on pie at tomorrow's lunch. And, if not, they'd be awfully good with some hot cocoa on Sunday evening.

As we boxed up everyone's desserts, Jackie asked me, "What are we planning on making for lunch tomorrow anyway?"

"How about roast chicken, green beans, mashed potatoes with gravy, and rolls?" I asked.

"That'll work." She handed Luis a white bakery box. "Anything we need from the grocery?"

"No. I believe we have everything we need." I stifled a yawn. "I'm glad. I definitely don't want to go shopping after work today."

"Looks like maybe you could use a nap, Amy-girl," Scott said.

"I could." I smiled and handed over his box of cookies. "But I'm afraid if I close my eyes, I won't wake up until morning."

"Would that be so bad?" he asked. Without waiting for an answer, he addressed Jackie. "I know Roger is short a man, so if he needs any help with the big house roof, have him give me a call."

"Have you done that sort of work before?" Jackie asked.

"Not roofing, but I've done handyman work. I'm confident I could figure it out."

"Hey!" I decided to mockingly chide him. "Don't go volunteering your services all over the place, mister. We need you here. You've already said you'd help with the cake tomorrow."

"Really?" Jackie squinted at Scott. "You're going to help decorate the parade cake?"

"You bet." He grinned.

"And have you ever decorated a cake before?" she asked.

"Jackie, Jackie, Jackie—things you've never done before are merely opportunities to learn and grow." He spread out the arm in which he wasn't holding the box. "Spread your wings!"

"No, thank you. As much as I'd like to see you covered in cake icing, I'll pass. After Sunday lunch, I plan to kick back on the sofa and binge watch TV until bedtime."

"Ah, she doesn't know what she'll be missing, does she?" Scott asked me.

I managed a smile. *I* didn't know what Jackie would be missing, and I was leery of finding out.

Chapter Ten

Before going home, I went to the big house to see how things were progressing on the roof. Roger was there working alone. I waved to him before noticing Clark Bennett's SUV in the driveway. Clark was Winter Garden's only resident physician; and although he and Mom had begun dating, I was mildly concerned to see his vehicle here so early. If he and Mom had a date, he shouldn't be here until later in the evening. I hurried inside.

"Is everything all right?" I asked when I saw Clark listening to Aunt Bess's heart. Placing the dessert box on the coffee table, I berated myself for asking such a stupid question. Of course, everything wasn't all right. "What's wrong with Aunt Bess?"

"Oh, now, don't worry about me." Aunt Bess winked. "I'm still kicking—for the time being anyhow. But I am thinking of making a new Pinterest board called *Things That'll Probably Kill Me*. I'm putting mold and mouse diseases at the top of the list. Do you think anybody has made pictures of mold and mouse diseases?"

"I'm sure someone has, Aunt Bess." Mom's exasperation was evident in her voice. "But, once again, those were not mouse droppings on your bed—those were cookie crumbs."

Aunt Bess harrumphed. "I reckon I'll have to add you to my board of things that'll probably kill me, given your hateful tone. Do you have a nice photo of yourself you can email me?"

"Yes," Mom said. "And you can make it the cover image for the board!"

"Mom, let's take this pie into the kitchen and give Aunt Bess some privacy with the doctor." I picked up the box.

"Pie? What kind of pie?" Aunt Bess asked.

"Pecan. And I promise it won't kill you." I bent and kissed her cheek.

"It might. I could eat it all and explode."

I was still trying not to laugh as I followed Mom into the kitchen. I knew Aunt Bess was on Mom's last nerve, but she certainly was a character. I made a mental note to remind myself of this day when sometime in the future Mom would be old and driving me up the wall.

After putting the pie into the refrigerator, I took Mom's hand and led her into the dining room. Although there was a small Christmas tree on a table in the living room, the main tree had traditionally been placed here in the dining room. Nana had liked it that way. There was plenty of room for everyone to get onto the floor and unwrap presents, and the tree could simply "spread out."

I'd helped Mom decorate the tree last week, and it was nice to take a minute now to revisit some of the ornaments—some of which had their better days behind them. The base of the tree was inside a red and gold box that looked like a toy drum.

I lightly touched a crocheted snowflake. "I remember the year you and Nana made these. They're so pretty and delicate."

"Yeah." She pointed out a dove. "I remember when Daddy carved this. I was just a little girl then, but I sat and watched him whittle it." She laughed as she took a lopsided Christmas tree ornament off the tree. It had been made with a popsicle stick painted green and a green pipe cleaner. Beads of various colors had been glued onto the tree. "You were so proud when you brought this home. Remember?"

"No." But I got reminded of it every year. Mom loved that ornament, as I was sure I'd love whatever ugly little trinket my child happened to bring home, if and when I had a child.

"What are you all looking at?" Aunt Bess asked, as she and Clark joined us in the dining room.

"This ugly little tree I made when I was in first grade," I said.

"Oh, now, don't feel bad," Aunt Bess said. "Jackie made her share of ugly stuff too." She walked around the side of the tree until she found a wreath my cousin had made. It was a wooden ornament she'd painted green, and there were three red dots on it— representing holly, I supposed. "Look at this. She got tired and quit. Blasted thing has three holly berries or red ornaments on it." She shook with laughter.

"Well, I hate to tell this on myself, but since we're sharing," Clark said, shaking his head. "One year, we decided to put our tree in the foyer rather than the living room like we had every other Christmas. That first night, I got up half awake to go downstairs for a glass of water. At the top of the stairs, I saw this huge shadow in the corner of the foyer. I called each of our daughters' names, but of course, neither answered."

Mom chuckled. She and Clark were still in the honeymoon phase of their relationship, and she found all his stories funny. But I had to admit, this one was proving to be pretty interesting.

"I crept closer, smacked the shadow—which, of course, turned out to be the tree—and knocked three of my wife's favorite crystal ornaments to the floor." He shrugged. "Broke them all to pieces. The sound brought everybody out of their beds to see what was going on."

"And was that what brought about your divorce?" Aunt Bess asked.

"No." He grinned. "We were already having problems, but the tree incident didn't help things by any means."

"I'm going out and checking on Roger," I said.

Walking outside, I looked up at the roof, shading my eyes with my hand. "What're you doing up there?"

"Fixing a roof. What're you doing down there?"

"I've been listening to Clark tell about the time he assaulted a Christmas tree. Want me to come up and help you?"

"That's a terrifying thought." He took off his gloves and left them on a stack of shingles. "Why don't I come down?"

As he climbed down the ladder, I said, "Scott said he'd be glad to help you if you need him. And I could call in Donna or Shelly to cover his shifts."

"Nah, I've about got it wrapped up," he said. "Thanks, though. Did I hear you right? Did you say Clark Bennett beat up a Christmas tree?"

"Only a little. It seems his wife's crystal ornaments got the worst of it."

His frown deepened. "Was that what he was trying to do—knock his wife's ornaments off the tree?"

"No. He forgot about the tree, came downstairs in the middle of the night, and it scared him," I said.

"Huh. And you're letting this guy date your mom?"

I laughed. "Yeah. I think he's fairly sane for the most part. We all do crazy stuff now and then."

"Yeah. I heard there was somebody planning to make a giant cake to haul on top of her car in the Christmas parade."

"Really? Who'd tell you something like that? Surely not someone who has refused to help."

"Yep." He put his hands on his hips. "So, what's up, Flowerpot? I know you didn't come out here to talk to me about Christmas trees and parade floats."

"I wanted to ask you if Sheriff Billings gave you a hard time about Devon," I said. "I mean, I know the sheriff can be a little intimidating at times, but he's a good man who's only trying to get to the truth."

"I know. He and Ryan are doing their jobs, that's all. They'd be remiss if they didn't question everyone involved with Devon, including Belinda."

"Belinda?"

Roger nodded. "Devon said Belinda had been really short with him lately, suspicious and accusatory."

"Did she think he was having an affair?" Her behavior toward Jackie crossed my mind.

"Not just that. He said she also accused him of hiding money from her—which I suppose he was, but it was only so he could buy her a special gift for Christmas."

"The necklace," I said. "Jackie told me about that. I hope Belinda and Devon didn't spend their last days arguing."

"I hope so too." His dubious expression told me we both thought the couple had done exactly that.

"Do you think Belinda could be responsible for Devon's death?" I asked. "I wouldn't know the first thing about sabotaging a car, but she might."

"All I know for certain is that I didn't do it." He jerked his head toward the ladder. "I'd better see how much more I can get done here while I still have plenty of daylight."

As I walked to my car, I hoped Roger had told the sheriff and Ryan how strangely Belinda Carpenter had been acting and what Devon had confided to him.

Chapter Eleven

When I got to my house, I saw that the cake dummies had been delivered and were stacked in boxes on my front porch. I packed the boxes into the car. They filled my entire backseat as well as the passenger seat of my Bug—the trunk was loaded with the fondant, food coloring, molds, and tools I'd bought the night before.

Eager to have everything in place so I could start decorating tomorrow after lunch, I drove the supplies to the café. I unlocked the door and then carried all my supplies back to the kitchen. I was opening the cake dummies when I heard a car outside.

Did I remember to lock the door back?

Hearing the door open, I realized I had not. It made me a little nervous since I was the only one there, but I thought it was most likely someone who saw my car outside and thought the café was open.

"Amy! Where are you?"

Dilly? I came from the kitchen to see that my ears hadn't deceived me. Dilly was standing in the dining room with one hand raised to her lips. "Hi, Dilly."

"Are you all right?" she asked.

"I'm fine. Are you?"

"Yes." She lowered her hand and gave me a sheepish grin. "I stopped because I saw your car, knew the café was closed, and I was concerned about you. You just never can tell these days, and I wanted to make sure you were okay."

"I appreciate your concern. I brought in the supplies I'll need—at least, I hope I have everything I need—to make the fake cake for the parade float. I'm planning on getting started tomorrow after lunch."

"You're making a float for the Christmas parade?" Dilly asked. "I hadn't heard a thing about it!"

"It kind of started out as a joke," I said, "but then a few of us got excited about the idea, and we decided to do it."

"I'd love to help, if there's anything I can do."

I gave her a broad smile. "How are you with clay?"

Frowning, she asked, "You mean, like modeling clay?"

I nodded. "If you can use modeling clay, you can use fondant." I explained that the tiers of the cake were going to represent the different types of foods served at the café. "I'm going to have cookies, pastries, burgers, hot dogs—"

"Chicken," she said. "You have to have a chicken leg."

"So, you're in?"

"I'm in. It sounds like such fun."

"Good," I said. "I'll need as many friendly faces around as I can get, especially since Ryan's mother is coming tomorrow."

Dilly screwed up her face. "My friend, Gladys Pridemore, can't stand Michelle Hall."

I didn't need Dilly to tell me that. I remembered all too well the women's fracas at the farmers' market.

"But don't you worry," Dilly continued, "I'm sure you'll be able to win Michelle over...you know, sooner or later."

"I'm not so sure I share your optimism, but I'll try to hold out hope nonetheless." Changing the subject, I asked, "Do you know any of the Carpenters who live—or lived—in Winter Garden? I'm asking because Devon was a Carpenter—he only moved back here from Florida when his aunt bequeathed some property to him."

"Carpenter..." Dilly mulled the name over.

"I thought maybe the family didn't appreciate their mother leaving Devon such a generous gift, but his cousin Chris said he didn't care. He told me the rest of the family got the good stuff."

"There used to be some Carpenters who lived over near Mill Creek," she said. "They owned all the land in that area and kept to themselves for the most part. Some people used to say some of the boys ran a still in the woods in back of their house, but I don't know personally whether that was true." She squinted up at the ceiling. "Every once in a while, we'd hear about one of the boys getting in trouble—they had the reputation of being mean." She brought her gaze back down to me. "You know, I hadn't thought about the Carpenters in years. I didn't even connect Devon to the family—probably because he didn't grow up around here."

Since Mom hadn't asked me to check in on Aunt Bess later and hadn't mentioned that Jackie was coming over, I determined that she must not have a date with Clark tonight. So when I got back home and saw that both Clark's SUV and Roger's truck was gone, I drove on up to the big house.

Mom knew immediately I had something on my mind. She opened the door asking, "Amy, is anything wrong?"

"No. I just want to speak with you and Aunt Bess alone," I said. "No date tonight?"

"Not tonight. Clark is taking one of his daughters to dinner and to do some shopping."

"That's nice." I arched a brow. "When are you going to take your daughter to dinner and to do some shopping?"

"Daughter, my foot!" Aunt Bess called from the living room, clearly overhearing our conversation as we walked in her direction. "Take me to dinner and shopping!"

"Why doesn't everyone gang up on me at once?" Mom asked. "That'd be terrific."

"What're you doing back up here already?" Aunt Bess pursed her lips. "You and Ryan haven't had a falling-out, have you?"

"No, I wanted to talk to you and Mom alone, that's all."

"Oh, well." She nestled into a more comfortable position on the sofa. "You've come to the right place for advice. Spill your guts."

"I was at the café—" I didn't want Mom and Aunt Bess to know about the cake until the big reveal. "—putting away some things when Dilly stopped by."

Aunt Bess tsked. "What was Dilly doing? Trying to get in your business? She's nice enough, but she can be as nosy as all get out."

"She saw my car and wanted to make sure I was okay," I said. "She knew the café was supposed to be closed."

"Oh...well...that was nice of her." Aunt Bess nodded. "Then what did you want to talk about?"

"I'm getting to that," I said.

Mom shot me a look of smug satisfaction—a *see what I mean* expression if I ever saw one.

Ignoring Mom, I told them about Dilly and me talking about the Carpenters. "She said she heard they used to have a still in the woods behind their house, but she didn't know if it was true or not."

"Goodness, yes, it's true!" Aunt Bess placed a hand on her chest. "Everybody in town knew that Old Man Haggerty, who used to walk up and down

Main Street drunk all the time, got his sour mash from the Carpenters. Like Dilly, though, I didn't connect Devon to that bunch."

"I can only remember one of the Carpenter boys from school," Mom said. "His name was Albert, but his friends called him Bertie. He was several years older than me, but we rode the school bus together. The way he'd stare at me always frightened me."

"I understand." I told them about how I caught Chris staring at me the night before in the restaurant. "Even when I caught him, he didn't look away. It sorta creeped me out, even though he's never been rude to me or anything. He simply had a way of looking at me that—"

"That felt more as if he was looking *through* you," Mom said, finishing my thought.

"Exactly."

"Maybe Chris is Bertie's son," she said.

"Should I relay all this information to Ryan?" I asked.

"Absolutely," Aunt Bess said.

"No," Mom said.

They'd spoken simultaneously, and I glanced from one to the other.

"You might be the very bird to crack this case wide open," Aunt Bess said.

"Or you might insult your boyfriend." Mom gave Aunt Bess a warning look, which Aunt Bess pointedly ignored. "Ryan and Sheriff Billings know their jobs very well. You don't want either of them to think you believe them to be incompetent."

"The police can't effectively solve crimes if they don't have all the information." Aunt Bess patted her hair. "That's why they rely on sleuths like us— angels, if you will—to provide a helping hand."

I gave them a tight smile and kept my mouth shut, not knowing whose advice I should follow.

That night when Ryan called, I didn't mention the investigation. I'd debated on whether to take the advice of Mom or of Aunt Bess; and when I heard Ryan's voice, Mom's warning won out. I wanted to contribute to solving Devon's murder and clearing Roger of any wrongdoing. But until I had information that was more than gossip or conjecture, I needed to stay out of Ryan's way and let him know I trusted him to get the job done.

Chapter Twelve

Rory woke me on Sunday morning by dropping his gingerbread man onto my face.

"Gee, thanks." I tossed the toy onto the floor, and he hopped off the bed to snatch it up. I considered pulling the covers over my head and trying to go back to sleep, but I knew that was pointless. For one thing, I'd already encouraged Rory's desire to play. For another, I had a lot to do today.

As I sat up, Rory brought the gingerbread man back. Once again, I pitched it to the other side of the room and watched him scamper after it. I sure hoped Ryan's mother never discovered what had become of the Christmas ornament she'd given me. She wasn't crazy about me as it was. Thinking I'd given her gift to my dog certainly wouldn't win me any points.

After feeding the pets, having a light breakfast, and getting myself ready, I went into the fancy room. I opened my laptop and searched for tutorials on using fondant to sculpt objects—foods, in particular. I wasn't disappointed. There were the most adorable doughnuts, fruits, hotdogs, cheeseburgers, tacos, carrots, corn, pancakes, and even a Thanksgiving turkey! I was delighted. Every item I could think of and type "fondant sculpted ____" into the search bar was there. We should have no trouble making the decorations for the dummy cakes as long as I took my laptop. I texted Scott and asked him if he could bring a laptop too, given that I was afraid we'd need more than one.

I went up to the big house and put the chicken in the oven. Since it would take well over an hour to roast, I had a few minutes before I needed to start the sides. I went into the living room and sat on the sofa beside Aunt Bess, who was working a crossword puzzle.

"Where's Mom?" I asked.

"Upstairs taking a bath. She's been in there forever. I hope she hasn't drowned." She paused. "I should add drowning to my *Things That'll Probably Kill Me* board."

I rose to go upstairs and check on Mom, but she was walking into the living room.

"Sit back down," she said, as she walked over to the armchair. "I'm fine."

"Good. I'd have hated to have had to add you to my *People I've Outlived* board." Aunt Bess tapped her pencil against her puzzle book. "What's a type of bird that begins with an *L* and ends with a *T*?"

"How many letters?" Mom asked.

She counted. "Eight. There's an E as the seventh letter."

I racked my brain. The only birds beginning with *L* I could think of were *lark* and *lapwing*, and neither of those fit.

"Lorikeet," Mom said.

"Lori who?" Aunt Bess scrunched up her face. "Lori Keet...is she the one who was in that show with the dad and the kids and the uncles and then she got in trouble over her kids' college?"

"A lorikeet is a type of parrot."

"How do you know that?" Aunt Bess asked her.

"I saw the birds on a documentary on TV the other night."

"When? I don't remember seeing it."

Mom blew out a breath. "You'd already gone to bed."

"And you were up with the TV going full blast?" Aunt Bess pressed her lips together and then filled in the word. "I don't know whether it's right or not, but it fits. *Lorikeet.* I've never in my life heard of that."

Figuring it would be a good idea to change the subject, I said, "I spoke with Ryan last night, but I decided to wait until I have concrete evidence for him before bringing up the subject of Devon's murder again."

"That's smart," Aunt Bess said, not looking up from her book. "Columbo used to always act befuddled until he was ready to spring the solution on the killer and have 'em arrested."

"Amy, why don't we work on lunch?" Mom stood. "That chicken smells so good, it's got me ravenous."

"I wonder where Jackie is," I said. "It's not like her to be this late."

"You're right. I'd better call and check on her." Aunt Bess got her phone from the end table. "What if we never really knew Roger at all, and now he's going around killing people? First Devon and now Jackie."

"You know that's not true," Mom said.

"I know it's probably not true." She called Jackie. "Where are you? Are you killed?"

Mom rolled her eyes at me as we continued to listen to Aunt Bess's side of the conversation.

"Huh. I'm sorry, sweetie. Want me to send you over some chicken soup or something? All right. I love you." Ending the call, she said, "She's not dead. She has the flu."

"Does she want the chicken soup?" I asked.

"No...but if we have enough chicken left over, I'd like some."

I called Jackie on my way to the café. She sounded stuffy and groggy when she answered.

"*Mwha--?*"

"You sound terrible," I said. "May I bring you anything?"

"No...it's...jusa code...hassa...run its course."

Code? She means cold. "All right. Get some rest and call me if you need me." After talking with Jackie, I called Roger but got his voice mail. "Hey, Roger, it's Amy. I'm worried about Jackie. She told me she has a cold, but Aunt Bess says it's the flu, and Jackie sounds really bad. I was wondering if you've seen her today and if there's anything I can do to help. Let me know. Thanks."

As I pulled into the Down South Café lot, I saw that Scott was already there. He was standing by the door holding his laptop bag, and he waved as I parked.

Quickly getting out of the car, I said, "I'm sorry, Scott—I thought you had a key!"

"I do." He held up his keyring as if I could determine by sight which key of many would unlock the door to the café. "But when I saw you coming, I waited to see if you needed help carrying anything inside."

"I appreciate your being so thoughtful, but I brought over everything we'll need yesterday." I unlocked the door, stepped inside, and flipped on the lights. "By the way, Jackie is sick and will be out of commission for a few days."

"Sorry to hear that," he said. "Anything serious?"

"Aunt Bess says it's the flu, but Jackie told me it was just a cold." I placed my laptop sleeve on the table. "Of course, Jackie was barely coherent when we spoke. I left a message for Roger. Hopefully, he'll give me a call back soon and provide all the pertinent details. Either way, I'm afraid we're going to be shorthanded this week." I unzipped the sleeve and removed the laptop. "I could call Shelly, but she hasn't worked much since her mom's Parkinson's diagnosis. I don't want to ask her unless I have to—I wouldn't want her to feel obligated."

"What about Donna?" As he spoke, he sat across from me and booted up his own laptop.

"I think Donna would be great, but I don't know if her kids are out of school on winter break yet. If they are, she'll probably have to decline."

"Text Luis," Scott said. "He'll know when the break starts if it hasn't already. If it has, maybe Oscar would be interested in working."

"That's a fantastic idea." Luis's younger brother, Oscar, had worked at the café some when we'd hosted the farmers' market, and he'd managed really well.

"I'm known for my brilliant mind, almost as much as for my striking looks." He waggled his eyebrows.

"And here I was thinking you were known for your humility."

"Doesn't that go without saying?" he asked. "So why do we need two laptops at a cake decorating party?"

I explained how I'd found the fondant sculpting tutorials online. "Anything you can dream up and type into a search engine, you can likely find it made of fondant. The tutorials will hopefully make our work faster and easier."

"And with two laptops, we can divide and conquer. How many of each item do you think we'll need?"

Before I could answer, Dilly bustled into the café and shrugged out of her jacket. "Walter stayed at his house watching the football game. He says he's not good at arts and crafts. Have I missed anything?"

"Not a thing," I said. "We're still getting set up and waiting for Michelle, Homer, and Dave Tucker—I called Dave about making our cake board." I caught a glimpse of a white pickup truck. "I think that's him now."

Dave Tucker walked in wearing khaki carpenter pants and a jean jacket over a white shirt. He had the energy of a man half his age. Rubbing his hands together, he said, "Hey there, Amy. Give me an idea of what we're doing here."

While I showed Dave my idea for the cake and Rosemary's instructions for the cake board, Homer and Michelle arrived. I was guessing he'd gotten there first because Michelle looked as if she still would rather be somewhere else. Oh, well...

"I've got the wood in my shop to get this done," Dave said. "I'll go ahead and get started on it. Do you need it back today?"

"Tomorrow will be fine," I said. "And if that doesn't work for you, then Tuesday will do."

"I'll get it to you as soon as I can." With that, he left.

Dilly clicked her tongue. "Walter had better be glad I met him before I met Dave Tucker."

I hid a smile. *Someone should make a reality show about Dilly and Aunt Bess and their adventures in dating. They could call it Dating Dowagers.*

"Who's your hero today, Homer?" I asked.

"Cake artist Duff Goldman." He smiled broadly. "I wanted to choose someone we can all relate to today."

"Are we going to get started soon?" Michelle looked at her watch.

"As soon as we hear a quote from Homer's hero." I nodded toward Homer.

After flicking a disparaging gaze toward Michelle, Homer quoted, "'The great thing about cake is it doesn't feel like work. You forget about work. Kids, adults, they all get the same look in their eye when they're decorating cakes... That's the magic right there.'"

"What a great quote to kick off our decorating session." I smiled.

"Yeah, man!" Scott punched the air with a fist. "We're gonna make some magic!"

Michelle rolled her eyes. I felt like telling her she could leave if she had somewhere else to be, but I didn't want to appear ungrateful for her offer of help. On the other hand, I was glad I had plenty of other volunteers so she didn't feel as if I had to rely on her.

"Very quickly, let me show you a mockup I made of our cake. I'm not an artist, but I think you'll get the idea." I passed around a sheet of paper on which I'd made a six-tiered cake and set out my ideas for each tier. "The sculpted foods will be placed on the top and the sides of their respective tiers because the people watching the parade go by will be seeing the sides of the cake. A yellow rosette border will separate the tiers and complement the bud vase that will sit on the top tier beside the coffee cup."

"I have an awesome idea for the coffee cup," Scott said. "We can use dry ice to make it appear that it's steaming."

I smiled. "The children will love it!"

"Speaking of the little ones," Dilly said, "you need to have someone walking beside the car on either side giving out candy or something."

"I hadn't thought of that," I said. "But it's an excellent idea."

"But not the same old stuff," Scott said. "You don't want to hand out candy canes like everyone else."

"What about tiny cookies?" Michelle asked.

My smile faded. "That sounds like a lot of work. To make and bag all those cookies would take up so much time. Besides, we're going to be short a person this week."

"Who?" Dilly asked.

"Jackie. She's got a bad cold." I didn't elaborate.

"That's too bad. I hope she's on the mend quickly." Dilly spread her hands. "But we'll worry about what to give out at the parade later. We'd better get started on making all these doo-dads to go on the cake."

We worked well that afternoon. I made coffee, we played—and sang along with—carols, and we made all the sculpted foods I thought I'd need for the cakes.

I was exhausted but pleased when I dragged into the house Sunday evening. I fed the pets and sank onto the sofa while I waited for the electric kettle to boil.

There was a knock on the door, and I half smiled as I rose, expecting it to be Ryan. Alas, he was not the Hall who was at my door—it was Michelle.

"Michelle—hi." I stepped back. "Please come in."

"I won't take but a minute because I know you're tired." She chuckled. "You're bound to be. I am, and I didn't work half as hard as you."

"Don't sell yourself short. You did a wonderful job. Thank you again for all your help." I gestured toward the kitchen. "Would you like some tea or hot chocolate? I have the kettle on."

"No, thank you. I need to be getting home soon. I keep thinking about those cookies, though, and what excellent publicity they'd be for the bakery. I'd be happy to—" She broke off, looking down at the floor.

Following her gaze, I saw Rory looking up at her adoringly. From his lips hung the gingerbread man.

"Oh, goodness!" I pretended this traitorous act was something I'd never seen before. "How did you get that off the tree?" I chased him, trying to get it.

Naturally, he thought we were playing and ran with it. The rascal hopped onto the middle of my bed, tail wagging. He dropped the toy onto my bed. I made a grab for it, but he scooped it back up and zoomed under the bed.

Red-faced, I returned to the living room without the ornament.

"Maybe hang it higher next time," Michelle said.

I nodded.

"Anyway, if you'd like to bake cookies later this week, I'd be happy to help."

"That'd be super," I said.

Chapter Thirteen

"It's not funny!" I exclaimed to a laughing Ryan on the phone later that evening.

"Yes, it is," he said, when he'd caught his breath. "Look, Mom made several of those ornaments, and I'll snag another one to replace the one Rory has adopted."

"Thanks. But that still doesn't help me with the cookies. Your mom is insisting that she and I make dozens of tiny sugar cookies to individually wrap and hand out at the parade. Do you know how much time that will take?"

"Aw, come on. It'll give you a chance to bond with her." He paused. "I'll even help—and referee—when I'm not working, if you want."

I had no response to that. I didn't want to make cookies with Michelle Hall as if we were June Cleaver and Wally's girlfriend. June would have been far more gracious. I imagined Michelle in a 1950s-style dress—maybe Amanda Tucker could make her one— pearls, and heels; but even with that visual, I couldn't erase the disapproving expression from the woman's face.

"What's tomorrow's special?" Ryan asked, breaking into my reverie.

"Um...it's pot roast. Be sure and let Sheriff Billings know—it's one of his favorite dishes."

"All right. And about Mom—"

Before he could finish that thought, Roger called.

"I'm sorry," I said to Ryan. "I have to answer this other call. It's Roger, and I've been waiting all day to ask him about how Jackie's doing."

"Okay. I love you, everything will be all right, and I'll talk with you tomorrow."

"I love you." As I switched over to Roger's call, I smiled at Ryan's words. Hearing him say he loved me would never get old. "Hi, Roger. How's Jackie?"

"She's resting right now. I'm sorry it took me so long to get back to you. I was at my parents' house when I got your message. I left, drove to Jackie's apartment, and then took her straight to the emergency room."

"Oh, no! I didn't realize she was that sick!" I felt like dirt. "I should've gone to check on her after leaving the big house."

"Don't beat yourself up, Flowerpot. She was diagnosed with a sinus infection. After getting her settled back in at home, I went and picked up her prescriptions and some sports drinks and soups. She's sleeping now."

"I am such a selfish jerk! I went straight to the café to work on the float instead of checking in on my cousin," I said. "When I called, she told me it was just a cold and—"

"Hush," he interrupted. "You two are cut from the same cloth, you know that? She was telling me she was sorry she had to let you down this coming week by not being able to work. I told her you'd probably have Shelly fill in."

"Her shifts are taken care of." I didn't tell him it was Oscar who'd be working in Jackie's place. That was likely to worry her even more. But since the county school system had already dismissed for the holiday break and Oscar was delighted for the opportunity to earn some money, it had worked out well. "May I ask you something about Devon?"

"Sure. But if it's 'did I cut the brake lines on his vehicle,' I hope you already know I didn't."

"It's not that. Chris and Adam seem really interested in whether Devon spoke much about his life in Florida—whether he missed it. I believe Adam wants Belinda to return to Florida."

"That might be the best thing for her since she has no family and very few friends here," he said.

"Did Devon seem to miss his old life?"

"He didn't like talking about Florida at all—wouldn't even discuss the Buccaneers' football game a few weeks ago. But I got the impression Belinda missed her old life. She'd mentioned it on a couple of occasions." He blew out a breath. "It struck me that she seemed bitter about being forced to *uproot her life and move to some little nowhere town*—her words, not mine. So, yeah, I think it would be good for her to move back."

Rory wandered into the living room, dropped his gingerbread man onto the floor, and leapt onto my lap. He licked my chin before settling in. I caressed his silky ears.

"What was the name of Devon's company?" I asked.

"I don't remember. I know it was a boat charter, but that's all."

"Let me know if you or Jackie need anything, all right? I can bring food for you guys to the big house tomorrow if you're still working on the roof."

"I should be finishing up tomorrow," he said. "But some food would be nice. Call me before you leave the café, and I'll let you know where I am. I appreciate your looking out for us."

"Hey, you're the one looking out for us! That roof nearly killed Aunt Bess, you know."

He chuckled. "She's gonna outlive us all. Saint Peter will have to knock her on the head with a hammer on Judgment Day."

After talking with Roger, I tried to snuggle up with Rory and watch TV, but I couldn't concentrate on the program. I went to the fancy room, got my laptop, and brought it back to the living room. By the time I'd booted up the computer, Rory was snoring softly at my side.

I did a search for boat charter companies in Florida. As you might imagine, the results were staggering. I added "Devon Carpenter" to the search. This time, the number of matches weren't as imposing, and they were more interesting.

One link was to a story in a South Florida newspaper about a smuggling boat. The article, dated May of last year, said in part:

A group of people from Haiti, Sierra Leone, China, and Jamaica paid thousands of U.S. dollars to reach South Florida. All the migrants were detained, as was the captain of the boat, Richard D'Angelo. D'Angelo was held on the charge of alien smuggling. The other boat captain, D'Angelo's partner Devon Murphy, leapt from the bow of the boat as Coast Guard boarded. Murphy was able to escape custody.

Devon Murphy. Devon Murphy. Devon Murphy. The name thumped in my head as if it were being played on some sort of internal drum. *Devon Murphy* couldn't possibly be *Devon Carpenter*, right? What fugitive on the run comes to Winter Garden, Virginia?

I did an image search for *Devon Murphy Florida boat charter.* And there he was—the man I knew as Devon Carpenter. He and his partner had appeared in a newspaper photo touting the business. A chill snaked down my spine.

I had to call someone. But who? Ryan? Roger?

Ryan. I'd start with Ryan.

My heart raced, as I waited for Ryan to answer.

"Couldn't wait until tomorrow to talk with me again, could you?" he asked, teasingly.

"Um...I have to ask you something."

"Amy, what's wrong?" His voice sounded stern and serious.

"It's about Devon Carpenter. Did you know he was using an alias?"

"I'll be right over," he said. "Have you spoken with anyone else about this?"

"No."

"Good. Don't." He ended the call.

While I waited for Ryan, I paced in front of the Christmas tree. Rory had woken up and was regarding me curiously, his little head turning this way and that.

"It's okay, baby," I assured him. "Everything's all right." Was I trying to comfort the dog or myself?

Princess Eloise didn't get off her perch until Ryan arrived—not because she was concerned about anything but because she loved him. She wound around his ankles before he sat with me on the sofa, and then she hopped onto the coffee table so she could observe him adoringly.

"Start at the beginning and tell me what you know and how you know it," Ryan prompted.

"All right. I was talking with Roger about Jackie, and then I asked Roger if Devon had spoken much about his life in Florida. Roger said he refused to talk about it at all but that he thought Devon's wife missed it."

"Why did you want to know about Florida?"

"Because Belinda's brother, Adam, keeps asking if Devon talked much about Florida and whether or not he missed it." I told Ryan Adam had asked me when he saw Sarah and me at the restaurant on Friday night, and then he came into the café on Saturday and was asking Homer about Devon.

"I saw him there on Saturday, but I didn't know what he was talking with Homer about." He frowned. "Why Homer?"

"I suppose he thought that as a regular, Homer knows most of the people who come in." I spread my hands. "He's right. And Devon had told Homer he should visit the Bahamas sometime."

"Okay. So, all this interest in Florida made you want to check out Devon's life there?" Ryan asked.

"Yeah. I wanted to see if I could find his former business. Was it successful? Why had he left? I mean, I figured it was unsuccessful if he was so willing to leave it and bring his wife here to live in Winter

Garden simply because he inherited a piece of property."

"True." Ryan sat back against the cushions, and Princess Eloise elegantly pounced onto his lap and gazed up at him with her beautiful blue eyes. He reached out, and she raised her head to meet his hand.

To be honest, I was a little jealous. She seldom ever paid me any attention other than at mealtimes.

"So, you knew?" I asked.

He nodded. "When we did a background check on Devon Carpenter, nothing came up. We found out then that his Social Security Number was fake. Devon Murphy was able to use the forged document to establish a new identity in Virginia."

"Did Roger know?" I held my breath.

"I don't think so. Upon learning that *Devon Carpenter* didn't exist, we did the same thing you did—searched online for a Devon who owned a boat charter service. We found *Devon Murphy* and contacted the Coast Guard."

"Is Devon's death related to his smuggling business then?" I asked.

"We don't know, and I can't tell you anything more about it," he said.

"Ongoing investigation—yeah, yeah, I know."

"You can't mention anything about this to Roger." He gently turned my head toward him. "All right? Promise me."

"I promise. You know I'd never compromise your investigation."

Chapter Fourteen

Upon arriving at the café on Monday morning, I was surprised to see Luis's car in the parking lot. I was accustomed to being the first one there. I went inside to the welcoming aroma of brewing coffee and found Oscar checking the napkin dispensers while Luis refilled the salt and pepper shakers.

"Wow, Luis, I'm going to have to step up my game to keep up with you," I said.

"Don't look at me." He jerked his head toward Oscar. "He insisted on getting here early."

Oscar grinned. "I wanted to make a good impression."

"Well, you certainly have. But you'd done that long before this morning. Still, I thank you both for your hard work." I went to the kitchen and put my purse in the cabinet. "Have you had breakfast?"

"Yes," Luis answered. "We had cereal at home."

As I got out a mixing bowl, I made a mental note to call Jackie sometime before the lunch rush to see how she was doing. Sifting flour into the bowl, I contemplated what I'd learned last night and wished I had someone to vent my feelings to—sometimes I found it difficult to gather my thoughts until I spoke them aloud. Of course, I could discuss what I was feeling with Ryan, but I didn't want him to think I was prying into his investigation.

But what I'd learned had been such a shock! Devon Carpenter had been using an alias—he wasn't who he'd claimed to be. Then again, he couldn't be lying about inheriting the property... could he? Was Devon really related to the Carpenter family, or was that kinship part of his ruse?

Adding baking powder to the flour, I decided to talk with Belinda. Not about what I'd learned, of course, but about Devon in general—his childhood, his former business, their life in Florida and how different that must be to living in Winter Garden. And since Jackie wouldn't be with me on this visit, Belinda might be more inclined to talk.

Just before noon, Dave brought the finished cake board. He'd done a terrific job.

"How much do I owe you?" I asked.

"Nothing. Let the cake board be my contribution to the Winter Garden Christmas parade," he said.

"Then at least let me give you lunch on the house."

He smiled. "That's a deal. I'll have some of that pot roast and cornbread you're advertising on your specials board."

I was bringing out Dave's plate when Sheriff Billings walked into the café.

Sitting at the counter beside Dave, he said, "I'll have some of that please."

"Coming right up." I returned to the kitchen to prepare the sheriff's food. When it was ready, I sat it in the window for Scott to deliver.

After giving Sheriff Billings his food, Scott came into the kitchen. "The sheriff wants a word with you after he's finished eating."

I huffed. "We're just about to hit the lunch rush!"

"I know. Maybe he wants to pay his compliments to the chef?"

"You and I both know that's unlikely."

He nodded. "Yeah, well... Remember what Guru Guy said this morning: 'While I am busy with little things, I am not required to do greater things.'"

I recalled Homer's hero today was Saint Francis de Sales. "What does that have to do with having to drop everything and talk with Sheriff Billings?"

"I don't know, but doesn't it sound good?"

I chuckled.

Scott pointed at my face. "There you go—I managed to get a smile out of you."

By the time Sheriff Billings was ready to speak with me, Luis, Oscar, and Scott were scurrying around the café trying to keep up with the hectic pace. I felt guilty asking Scott to take over in the kitchen.

The sheriff was standing by the door leading to the patio—which was closed to the public during the winter—and he motioned for me to join him there. We stepped outside.

"Molly and I are looking forward to the Christmas parade. Ryan has told us all about this cake you're making." He leaned closer. "I know you're busy, so I'll make this quick. I'm impressed you were able to discover Devon Carpenter's secret almost as quickly as we did. And I know we can trust you to keep the information to yourself."

"Naturally," I said.

"I realize you must have a million questions. So do we. We're diligently seeking answers, and you'll know everything as soon as an arrest has been made."

In other words, *Mind your own business—you'll know when everyone else does.* "Do you have a solid suspect then?"

"Not yet. Just..." He examined my face, and I thought he softened slightly. "Concentrate on the float you're making. That cake is going to be the talk of Winter Garden for months to come."

I nodded. There it was—*be a good girl and make your float.* He didn't really mean any harm by that. He simply meant that as a civilian I shouldn't worry about the case.

But I knew Belinda Carpenter—or whatever her real name was—wouldn't talk with the police. If, as I suspected, Devon's death had to do with whatever he'd left Florida to escape, she'd be terrified that she'd be killed next. I certainly would be if I was in her position. Since I knew the Florida police were searching for Devon in connection to the alien smuggling, I didn't believe Belinda would feel very trusting toward the Winter Garden Police Department. And, yet she might very well confide in a café owner who merely came to check on her and bring her food.

Ryan had been in the café not long after Sheriff Billings had left and had brought me another gingerbread man ornament. My hope was that Michelle would see it hanging on the tree when she arrived and think I'd rescued the one she'd given me from Rory and brought it here for safekeeping—and to proudly display. Very proudly. Would've shone a spotlight on the thing if I had one.

As if Michelle would be so easily fooled.

Everyone else had gone by the time she arrived. I came from the kitchen to find her looking at the tree. I stupidly thought the plan had worked. I was even gloating a little to myself. Until...

"Why is Ryan's gingerbread man here instead of hanging on his tree at home?" she asked. "Didn't he like it? Did he feel the ornament was too juvenile for a grown man's tree?"

"It was nothing like that." I hurried over, anxious to smooth over her ruffled feathers. "I told Ryan what happened yesterday with Rory, and he brought me this one."

Her face stiffened. "I see. You allowed yours to get ruined, so my son brought you his. Apparently, you didn't think I'd notice the difference; but that one's eyes are brown. Yours has navy blue eyes."

"We weren't trying to pull anything over on you." Sure, we were, and she knows it.

Shrugging slightly, she said, "I should've asked you both if you wanted the ornaments before I went to the trouble of making them. I never intended to saddle either of you with something you didn't want."

"I think they're adorable, and I'm sure Ryan treasures his too. In fact, I'm going to insist he take his ornament back home to his tree where it belongs," I said. "I know he wants very much for the two of us to get along. That's why he allowed me to borrow this little gingerbread man."

She lifted the quilted tote she'd carried inside with her. "I found some darling gift bags today that will be perfect for your mini cookies, and I made some tags with your logo on them to tie the bags closed."

"How thoughtful." I smiled. "Thank you."

Brushing aside my gratitude, she said, "We should get started. By my calculations, if we make seventy-five mini cookies each evening this week, we'll have three-hundred-seventy-five to hand out during the parade."

I felt my knees weaken. "You and I are going to make seventy-five cookies each day after work?"

"I don't see how else we're going to reach our quota by Saturday, do you?"

I wondered if the smile I managed to plaster onto my face looked as fake as it felt. Michelle Hall had decided the Down South Café was handing out mini cookies at the parade when I'd have been perfectly satisfied tossing bubblegum or lollipops into the crowd. While she had an excellent point about giving people something unique with a tie-in to the café, I hadn't intended to get roped into spending all my afternoons this week with my boyfriend's disapproving mother.

Chapter Fifteen

It was already dark outside by the time I'd taken Roger and Jackie their supper and gotten to the big house with food for Mom and Aunt Bess.

"Lord, have mercy! Where've you been?" Aunt Bess asked. "My belly was afraid my throat had been cut I've not eaten in so long."

"Sorry." I kissed her cheek and turned to leave.

"Wait," Mom said. "Where are you going?"

"I have an errand to run, and then Ryan and I are watching TV at my house later."

"Well, thank you for dinner," she said.

"You're welcome," I called over my shoulder.

I desperately wished I'd been able to sit down with Mom and Aunt Bess and tell them why I'd been late with dinner. They'd probably figured I spent too much time with Jackie and Roger to stay and chat with them, but that hadn't been the case. I'd dropped off their food, expressed relief when Jackie told me she was feeling better, assured her I didn't want her coming into work for the rest of the week, and left. I wasn't about to tell my cousin and her boyfriend, the suspect, that I was going to see Belinda.

But I couldn't tell Mom and Aunt Bess about Michelle and the cookies without ruining my surprise about the float. Not only did I want them both to be blown away by the cake, I didn't want them second-guessing my design choice—especially now that so much of the preliminary work had been done. Nor did I want the float mentioned on social media before its reveal at the parade. Naturally, Aunt Bess would be posting it on one of her Pinterest boards in the car on the way home from the parade, but that would be fine. I let my mind wander to which board she'd post it to: *Things I'd like to Eat But Won't Fix*, *Lord, Have Mercy*, or—heaven forbid—*Crime Scenes*.

I left the big house, drove to Belinda Carpenter's place, and checked my watch. I had around forty minutes—provided she didn't turn me away at the door—before I had to get back home, feed the pets, and make some snacks before Ryan arrived. The rumbling of my stomach at the thought of snacks reminded me that I hadn't eaten since the jelly biscuit I'd had after the lunch rush.

Relief washed over me when I saw that Belinda was home and willing to let me inside. She took the bakery bag I offered her, and I followed her into the kitchen.

"I thought you might be tired of sweets and casseroles," I said. "I've brought macaroni and cheese, mashed potatoes, ham biscuits, and green beans."

"Thank you awfully much, but you didn't have to do this. You've already brought plenty of food."

"Well, I know that although Devon has got family here in Winter Garden, you don't... except for your brother, and I know he's only here temporarily." I glanced toward the living room. "I brought enough food for him too. He hasn't gone back to Florida yet, has he?"

Grinning smugly, she asked, "Is that what this is about? You're sweet on my brother?"

"Not at all," I said. "I just wanted to make sure you're holding up all right. You gave me a scare when you ran out of the café the other day."

"Oh. That." She gestured for me to have a seat. "I'm doing better now."

Pulling out a chair, I sat and folded my hands on my lap. "As I said before, it must be hard not having all your family and friends here to rally around you. Are you planning to sell and move back to Florida?"

Belinda lifted and dropped one shoulder. "I don't know what I'll do yet. I'm feeling a tug in that direction, though. Without Devon here, I don't have much of a reason to stay."

"Are you close with the Carpenters?"

"Not really. Chris is the only one I've been around much, and he seldom has much to say to me," she said. "He's the one Devon bought—I mean, took the house over from when he inherited it."

She definitely said bought. A faux pas, but one worth looking into. Still, I shouldn't press the matter now. "Chris and Adam seem to be getting along well. They were in the café together on Saturday." I didn't mention that Sarah and I had also seen them together on Friday.

"Yeah, Adam's trying to talk Chris into coming to Florida and running charters with him." A flicker of fear registered in Belinda's eyes before she asked, "Would you like something to drink? I have a fresh pot of coffee made."

"No, thanks. I really should be going. What's that old saying—miles to go before I sleep?" I stood. "Anyway, call or come by the café anytime."

As I got into my car, I wondered if Adam Tate had been a partner in Devon and Richard D'Angelo's charter business. I'd have asked, but after Belinda slipped up and told me Adam was trying to recruit Chris, I knew her guard was up and that she wouldn't tell me anything else of value. But she *had* told me enough to send me back to the search engines.

Ryan dipped a tortilla chip into the queso. "This is really good. I'm glad you decided to go with appetizer-type foods rather than a heavy meal."

"Me too." I didn't feel the need to say I did the best I could with the amount of time I had. He and I were both enjoying the food, and that's all that mattered.

Having finished his own dinner long ago, Rory proudly trotted out of the kitchen with the gingerbread ornament.

"He does love that thing, doesn't he?" Ryan grinned. "I've never seen him so taken with a toy."

"Neither have I. Normally, he'd have torn the thing to shreds immediately, but he treasures that little thing. I wish I could tell your mother how much Rory appreciates it, especially since she thinks neither of us do." I told him about her reaction at seeing his ornament on the tree at the café. "It's in my purse. Don't let me forget to give it back to you before you leave. If she comes in tomorrow and sees that it isn't on the café tree, I'd like to be able to tell her it's back where it belongs."

"She's coming back tomorrow?" he asked.

"Oh, yes. Today's cookie-baking marathon was the first of five. We're doing one every evening this week leading up to the parade on Saturday."

He laughed. "That's hilarious."

"You think it's so funny, you can take my place tomorrow," I said.

"And you'll work on the investigation?"

"I'm already ahead of you on that."

That wiped every smidgeon of the smile from his face. "Amy, what did you do?"

"I paid a visit to Belinda Carpenter a little while ago." I decided I needed a tortilla chip with queso myself. It beat answering the questions I knew were coming.

"I know you didn't tell her anything you learned about Devon. You'd never do that." He sounded confident, but there was a teensy thread of doubt beneath his words.

"Of course not. I was there to get information, not give it. All I gave was food to a grieving widow." I gave him what I hoped was an innocent, downright wholesome look.

"And did you get any information?"

"Belinda gave me the pickaxes, but we have to mine the gold. Let me get my laptop." I retrieved my computer from the fancy room and booted it up. "Do you know how Devon is related to the Carpenters?"

"Yes. Do you?"

"No, but there's no need to hedge on the answer since it's not directly relevant to your investigation, and we'll save time if I don't have to search for the Carpenter family tree online."

"Fine," he said. "Devon's mother was the sister of the Carpenter matriarch."

"The matriarch." That word fired up all my neurons. "If Devon's mother married into the Carpenter family, then that surname wouldn't show up in his background at all. It was the perfect choice for an alias. It would be like me calling myself Amy Fonseca. Unless the authorities knew about my relationship with Jackie, they'd never make a connection between Amy Flowers and Amy Fonseca. Brilliant."

"Well, I'm glad you have the perfect alias now in case you have to go on the lam."

"Oh, it wouldn't work for me because you and Sheriff Billings know Jackie is my cousin. I'd have to come up with something else." I smiled. "But that's not something I have to worry about—not right now, anyway."

"You know, you're more like your Aunt Bess than you realize sometimes." He frowned slightly, making me feel that what he was saying wasn't necessarily a compliment. Okay, it wasn't a compliment, but I decided to take it as giving credit where credit was due. Aunt Bess was a pretty smart cookie.

"The reason I wanted to know about Devon's connection to the Carpenter family is because when I was talking with Belinda she slipped up and said Devon *bought* their house from Chris. She quickly backtracked, but I feel we should determine whether the property was bought or inherited. Catching her in a lie like that could force her to tell you the real reason she and Devon came to Winter Garden."

"Or we could simply confront her with what we know," Ryan said. "We've been lining our ducks up to do exactly that."

"Why slam a horsefly with a sledgehammer when a swatter would be every bit as efficient and no way near as messy?" I clicked around online until we were able to determine that the Carpenter property was indeed sold rather than bequeathed.

"But what does that tell us?" He dug back into the queso.

"Not much on its own, but Belinda also told me Adam is hoping to get Chris to become a partner in the charter business. I suggest we find out if Adam was a partner in Devon's venture from the start or if Adam started his own business after Devon left town."

After an extensive online search, we discovered that Cyrus Carpenter was an officer in the charter company helmed by Devon Murphy and Richard D'Angelo.

"Adam merely picked up the slack caused by Devon's departure," Ryan said. "The Carpenters have been involved in this smuggling business all along."

"It makes me wonder if Devon planned to go back to Florida and resume operations when the heat died down. Could that be why Adam was asking everybody if Devon had mentioned anything about Florida to them?"

He gently closed my laptop. "I believe the main thing I need to do is to determine who among the Winter Garden Carpenters is involved in this smuggling operation and to what extent. But that can wait. We shouldn't waste the rest of tonight on an investigation we can't pursue until tomorrow."

Chapter Sixteen

Bryson Neal came into the café to have breakfast on Tuesday morning. After placing his order for eggs over easy, bacon, rye toast, and grits, he asked Scott, "How's the float coming along?"

"Dude, it's amazing! A bunch of us worked on it Sunday afternoon and—"

I stuck my head through the window into the dining room and cut Scott off. "And we're planning to have someone walk on either side of the car and hand out mini, individually-wrapped cookies." I didn't want Scott giving too much away about our cake. That way, if things didn't go according to plan and I had to make some last-minute changes, no one except my volunteers would be the wiser.

"I think handing out cookies is a swell idea," Bryson said. "It'll give parade-goers a reason to hurry on into the café and get more cookies."

Laughing, I said, "That's the general idea."

"I'm glad things are going so well," he said.

Scott poured Bryson some coffee. "Like me, you don't seem to have quite the drawl that many people around here have. I moved to Winter Garden from New Mexico to be closer to my mom and sister."

"That's cool." Bryson shook a couple of sugar packets before emptying them into his coffee. "I was an Army brat—grew up everywhere and nowhere, if you know what I mean."

Homer walked in and overheard what Bryson had said. "My hero of the day also moved around a lot as a child because his father was in the Canadian Armed Forces." He smiled and took a seat beside Bryson. "That hero is Michael J. Fox, and I'm Homer Pickens."

"Glad to meet you, Mr. Pickens. I'm Bryson Neal, the town manager. I'm from Northern Virginia initially, but my wife and I fell in love with this area on vacation and decided to relocate. I was able to land my job before we sold the house up north, but sadly, my wife hasn't found work she enjoys yet."

"Mr. Fox once said there's always failure, loss, and disappointment," Homer said. "'But the secret is learning from the loss and realizing that none of those holes are vacuums.' I'm sure your wife will have more luck finding a job after the holidays."

"I think so too, Mr. Pickens," Bryson said. "I've told her to relax and enjoy the holidays."

"Homer, I'll have your sausage biscuit ready in a minute; and Mr. Neal, your breakfast is coming up," I said, heading back to the grill.

Scott had delivered Bryson Neal's breakfast to him, and he was eating while listening to Homer extol the wisdom of Michael J. Fox when I brought out Homer's sausage biscuit.

"Another clever remark Mr. Fox once made was: 'I am careful not to confuse excellence with perfection. Excellence I can reach for; perfection is God's business.' Don't you think that's a good one?"

"Brilliant, Guru Guy!" Scott gave Homer a thumbs-up.

Belinda Carpenter walked into the café and gazed around the dining room before fixing her eyes on Bryson. Her hand flew to her throat.

"Belinda, good morning," I said. "It's nice to see you. May I get you a menu?"

She nodded. "Y-yes, please."

"Mrs. Carpenter, how are you holding up?" Bryson asked.

"F-fine, thank you." Belinda slid into a seat at a table to the right of the counter. As it was a slow time of day, there weren't many other patrons there.

I took Belinda a menu and offered her some coffee.

"Some of that French vanilla would be wonderful," she said.

"Have you given any thought as to what you'll do going forward?" Bryson left the now that Devon is gone part of his question implied.

"I...um...I'm considering moving back h-home...to Florida." With a trembling hand, Belinda brushed her hair back from her face.

"Belinda, are you all right?" I poured the French vanilla coffee into her cup.

"Oh, yes. I-I'm fine. Just all the stress I've been under." She tried to smile.

"Do you think some pancakes might help?" I asked. "Or an omelet maybe?"

She pointed at the menu. "One of those cinnamon rolls would hit the spot."

"You've got it." As I hurried back toward the kitchen, I heard Homer share a bit of encouragement with Belinda.

"Mrs. Carpenter," he said, "the talented actor Michael J. Fox once said, 'I truly believe that we have infinite levels of power that we don't even know are available to us.' I hope you're able to draw on your powers and find some strength and comfort today."

"You and me both," Belinda said. "You and me both."

When Michelle arrived at the end of the work-day—or what, for the time being anyhow, had become the *middle* of my workday—I was standing at the counter spreading shortening onto the largest cake dummy.

She crinkled her brow as she strode over to inspect my work. "What are you doing?"

"Preparing the cake dummy for the fondant. I'm hoping to get the first two tiers covered and stacked today while you work on the cookies." I didn't bat an eye, even though I knew Michelle wouldn't be happy with my plan.

Last night as I'd lain in bed exhausted but unable to sleep, I'd had an epiphany—this was my café, my kitchen, and my float. I'd committed to creating a giant cake, not to making three-hundred-seventy-five cookies. Since the cookies were Michelle's idea, I felt she should be the one primarily responsible for them. If she didn't understand that, she could give up on the project, and I could have my volunteers hand out regular candy like everyone else. Granted, the cookie idea had been inspired, but it was an expensive and time-consuming giveaway.

"This is going to be the table tier," I said. "How do you think I should do the tablecloth?"

Tilting her head this way and that, she said, "I think it would be pretty if you could scallop the tablecloth to show the texture of the table underneath."

"That's an excellent idea. I bought a wood grain fondant texture mat to use for the table, so I definitely want to show that off." I picked up the mat to show Michelle.

She grinned. "This is fun. I'll get started on the cookies. You make the table and then we'll worry about the tablecloth."

"Deal." She was taking my independent streak much better than I'd thought she would. "When the cookies are cool enough to bag, I'll take a break and help. I made some labels listing ingredients and allergy warnings before work this morning, and we can add those to the bags too."

"What a super idea. I'm sorry I didn't think of it myself." She went on into the kitchen and got to work.

Who was this woman? And what had she done with the Michelle Hall who didn't like me and didn't seem to want me dating her son?

Setting those questions aside for the moment, I put on gloves and put some gel color onto a ball of white fondant. For a couple of minutes, I completely lost myself in tinting the fondant. Squeezing and kneading a ball of fondant was pretty therapeutic. Maybe Belinda Carpenter should give it a try. She certainly had been wound as tight as a watch this morning. I understood her pain, but this was more of a fear. Was she afraid the person who'd killed her husband would come after her? She had to be!

"Michelle, I could use some advice," I called into the kitchen.

"Sure. Is it about the cake?"

"No. It's about your son."

She stopped dropping cookie dough onto the cookie sheet and returned to the counter. "What about him?"

I wanted to ask her whether she thought I should tell him about Belinda's behavior and how I thought Belinda was frightened of Devon's killer. But I chickened out. Instead, I asked, "Could you please give me an idea on what to get Ryan for Christmas? I haven't got a clue."

"Let me think about it while I'm finishing this first batch of cookies, and we'll talk it over while we bag them up."

As I rolled out my tan fondant into a thirty-two-inch circle, I wondered what Michelle would advise me with regard to Ryan's present. I really didn't know what to get him, but I'd take any suggestions his mother made with a grain of salt. I imagined her telling me to get him gym socks or a pair of gloves. *Yeah, romantic stuff there, Mrs. Hall.*

It struck me that gloves might actually be a great gift for Ryan. He was out in all kinds of weather. But, again, not terribly romantic.

I was finishing up texturizing the fondant when Michelle came out of the kitchen again.

"It smells great in there," I said.

"Smells good in here too. Wonder how many parade-goers will want a piece of that fake cake?"

"I can almost guarantee my Aunt Bess will. And she won't believe me when I tell her it's not real."

She laughed. "Ryan says she's a sight."

"She certainly is."

Michelle waited while I positioned the fondant onto the cake and cut off the excess.

"What do you think?" I asked.

"Looks like a tabletop to me." She jerked her head toward the kitchen. "Do you have time to help bag some cookies? If not, I can handle it."

"No. I could use a break from the fondant for a few minutes." I followed her into the kitchen and put on a fresh pair of gloves.

"Ryan has been wanting to learn guitar," she said, as she unpacked the cellophane bags, ties, and labels from her tote. "Has he spoken to you about it?"

"No." He hadn't. Of course, I was now wondering why he hadn't. Did he genuinely want to learn guitar, or had he said something in passing to his mother like, *I'd like to learn to play guitar one of these days* without knowing how seriously she'd take the comment? Or maybe he wanted to learn to play guitar and then surprise me with how well he could play.

"David and I are planning to buy him a guitar for Christmas." She, too, put on a fresh pair of gloves. "You could maybe get him some personalized picks and a gift certificate for some lessons."

"That sounds better than what I was considering," I said. "I was leaning toward some nice leather gloves."

She scoffed. "Darling, leave the gloves to his grandmother. You're his girlfriend, for goodness' sake!"

Chapter Seventeen

After finishing up at the café, I took the ingredients for chicken Alfredo over to Jackie's apartment. The dish was one of her favorites.

She looked better when she opened the door to her apartment. Rather than the robe she'd been wearing yesterday, she wore a pair of navy lounge pants and a white, waffle-knit sweater.

"How are you feeling?" I asked, as I walked through to the kitchen with the bag of groceries.

"Much better. I don't know that I'm up to working a full day yet, but—"

"No," I interrupted. "The doctor said you should take the week off, and you're going to do it."

She waved the doctor's orders away with a flip of her hand. "What does he know? I'll go crazy if I have to stay in here watching television for another day."

"Then don't watch TV. Look into those online classes you mentioned." I retrieved a pot from Jackie's cabinet and filled it with water.

"I guess I could do that," she said.

"Where's Roger?" I asked. "Will he be here soon?"

"Nope. He's at his parents' house helping his dad install a new water heater. He's eating there this evening and said he'll call me when he gets home."

"Up for a little company then?" Even though it had only been a couple of days, I'd missed talking with her.

"Definitely. I spoke with Granny earlier, and she told me she and Aunt Jenna were going shopping."

I nodded. "Those two seemed to be looking forward to their outing—I hope they'll be as happy when they get back home."

"Me too," she said, with a chuckle. "But they're having dinner, and Granny said they might see a movie while they're out, so they should be fairly content."

Holding up my crossed fingers, I reiterated that I hoped so.

Jackie sat down at the table. "So, how are things going at the café? Does everyone miss me?"

"You know they do." I got out a skillet for the chicken. "Belinda Carpenter came in today, and she acted so weird."

"That woman hasn't acted in a way I'd describe as normal through this entire ordeal." She frowned. "What did she do this time?"

"Mr. Neal and Homer were trying to talk with her, and she was stammering and trembling." The water came to a boil, and I dumped in the pasta. "I realize everyone grieves differently, but Belinda didn't appear to be sad—she seemed frightened."

"Well, that's understandable. Maybe she's afraid the police suspect her of Devon's murder. Or she could think she'll be next."

"That makes sense." I put olive oil in the skillet and added the chicken. "If Belinda didn't kill her husband, then she probably at least believes she knows why he was killed. She might even know who did it."

She shuddered. "That whole situation gives me the creeps. Leave the investigating to the cops, Amy."

"I will. But it wouldn't hurt to tell Ryan what I'm seeing in Belinda's behavior."

Gayle Leeson

Obviously ready to change the subject, Jackie asked, "How are things going with Ryan's mom? Did she show up for cookie duty again today?"

"She did." I stirred the pasta and turned down the heat before turning toward Jackie. "In fact, I turned the cookie-making over to her while I worked on the cake."

Her mouth formed an O before she laughed. "And how did *that* go over?"

"Better than I'd anticipated," I said. "I was able to get the two bottom tiers completed, and I helped Michelle bag up the cookies. She even gave me an idea for what to get Ryan for Christmas."

"And what did she suggest?"

Smiling, I turned back to flip over the chicken strips. "I was skeptical too at first. But she mentioned that she and David are getting Ryan a guitar because he told them he'd been wanting to learn to play. She mentioned that I could get him a gift certificate for lessons."

"Uh-huh. Has Ryan ever shown any interest in learning guitar to you?"

"No...and I considered that."

"I'm not saying Michelle would deliberately set you up," Jackie said. "But you know me—I'm not the most trusting person in the world. If I were you, I'd do a little digging before getting Ryan something he might not want."

"That's a good idea. I'll feel him out about it after I talk with him about Belinda Carpenter."

I dropped by the police station on my way home from Jackie's apartment. Sheriff Billings was there, and he came out to stand by Ryan's desk when he saw me enter the building.

"Hey there, Amy!" he called.

Ryan spun his chair around to give me a wink. "Hi."

"Hi. Have you fellows had dinner?" I asked.

"We have, but what have you got?" Sheriff Billings asked.

I laughed. "Nothing, but I'll be happy to go get you something if you're hungry."

"Aw, we're not—at least, I'm not." The sheriff patted his flat stomach.

"But we'd have been willing to make a little room if you had brought something," Ryan said, with a grin.

Although initially I'd have rather not spoken with Sheriff Billings present, I decided to go ahead and tell them both about Belinda Carpenter—better to talk it out now than to have the sheriff thinking Ryan had been discussing the investigation with me inappropriately.

"Belinda Carpenter was in the café today," I said. "You know, she acts more like a woman afraid than a woman grieving the loss of her husband."

"Amy—" Sheriff Billings began.

"I'm well aware neither of you are at liberty to discuss ongoing investigations," I interrupted. "And I'm not here to talk about Devon's murder case. I only want to report an observation about Belinda's behavior. Isn't it a reasonable assumption to say you see suspects when they're on their guard?"

The sheriff gave me a brief nod. "Fair enough."

"Belinda has been into the café on two occasions recently, and her conduct has gone from bad to worse." I explained about the time she left in tears. "That, I could understand. After all, she is—I hope—grieving the loss of her husband. But when she came in today, she was frightened. Her hands were trembling, she was stammering, and she was telling Bryson Neal, of all people, that she was considering leaving Winter Garden and returning to Florida."

"Bryson Neal," Ryan said. "He's the new town manager, isn't he?"

"Right. He's the one who came by and asked me to make a float for the Christmas parade," I said. "He came in today to have brunch and to check on our progress."

Frowning, Ryan asked, "Wonder if he checks up on all his float builders?"

"I don't know." I shrugged. "Maybe he was hungry, and the float was all he knew to talk about with me and my staff."

"Did he seem to know Belinda?" Sheriff Billings asked.

"He did. He called her *Mrs. Carpenter* and asked how she was holding up." I struggled to recall more of their conversation. "And I think he wanted to know what her plans were."

Ryan began typing on his keyboard. "Does Belinda Carpenter work anywhere?"

"I don't think so." The sheriff looked up at the ceiling. "I believe she used to be a server in a restaurant in Abingdon, but she quit."

Reading from his computer screen, Ryan said, "You're right—she's currently unemployed."

"Still, couldn't the restaurant be where she knows Mr. Neal from?" I asked.

Gayle Leeson

Sheriff Billings raised his brows. "You're here to report an observation, not to participate in the investigation, remember? If Deputy Hall and I need to discover Belinda Carpenter's relationship to Bryson Neal—if there is one—we'll do the legwork."

I held up my hands in mock surrender.

"However," he continued, "if you see any more reportable behaviors, I trust you'll let us know."

"You know I will," I said.

"And if you have any cookies or cakes or pies you need taste-tested, we'll be happy to help with that too." He grinned. "Now I'll leave you two lovebirds alone."

I waited until Sheriff Billings got back to his office. "Oh, shucks. I meant to tell him tomorrow's special."

"I can tell him," Ryan said. "What is it?"

"Turkey casserole, but I should tell him myself. You know, let him know there's no hard feelings about his shutting me out of the discussion about Belinda and Mr. Neal."

He looked suspicious, but he didn't question my motives.

"Be right back." I hurried to Sheriff Billings' office.

Scratching his head, he asked, "Has somebody been behaving strangely already? Is it Hall?"

"No. Well, maybe..." I quietly explained about Michelle's gift suggestion.

"I don't rightly know," he said. "But give me a day or two, and I'll be able to report back. It's the least I can do."

"Thanks." I grinned. "Oh, and tomorrow's special is turkey casserole."

"I like turkey casserole. Put me some aside please."

When I returned to Ryan's desk, he squinted at me. "That took longer than I expected."

"He told me to put him some aside," I said. "Would you like some too?"

"Absolutely." He took my hand. "You could simply ask me, you know."

"Ask you what?" I tried to look innocently perplexed.

"What I want for Christmas."

With a squeak of indignation, I walked away. His laughter followed me all the way to the door.

Chapter Eighteen

On Wednesday morning, I went into the café, prepared the coffee pots, and pre-heated the oven for doughnuts. As I was getting my two favorite mixing bowls from the cabinet, Scott came in.

"Morning, Amy! What are you making this morning?"

"Cinnamon sugar doughnuts." I used non-stick cooking spray on my doughnut pans.

"How can I help?" he asked.

"Want to whisk together the dry ingredients while I'm combining the wet?"

"Sure." He got each of us a whisk. "I love cake doughnuts."

"Me too."

"May I buy a couple of these bad boys before you put them on display? I know they'll go fast."

I grinned. "No, you may not buy the bad boys. But you can set aside as many as you want as soon as they're done. That's one of the many perks of working here."

"She should be happy with two." He ducked his head and measured flour into the bowl.

He should've known better than to think I'd let that *she* slide. "She who?"

"Um...Ivy."

"Are you sure we're talking about your sister?" I asked. Ivy didn't strike me as the type who went cuckoo over doughnuts.

"Positive—she's the only Ivy I know." He added baking powder, baking soda, and salt.

I tilted my head. "There's something you're not telling me."

"I'm not supposed to tell, Amy-Girl!" His eyes widened before he looked away to grab the cinnamon.

"If you have a secret, I understand," I said. "You have to keep your word."

"Do you promise not to say anything to anyone else?"

"Of course!" I bit my lip. "But if you're not supposed to tell, I don't want you breaking a confidence on my account."

"I don't think she'd mind my telling you." He measured cinnamon into the bowl. "At least, not as long as you don't tell anyone else."

"You're about to burst at the seams, aren't you?" I laughed.

"Yes! She's going to have a baby!"

I squealed. "Oh, my gosh! You're going to be an uncle!"

"I know!"

"The coolest uncle ever!" I put down my whisk and hugged him. "I'm so happy for Ivy—and you!"

"Me too!" He gave me a squeeze. "She doesn't want many people to know until she's through her first trimester."

I pretended to lock my lips. "Her secret is safe with me."

The morning rush was over by the time Sheriff Billings came in for breakfast. He came up to the counter, caught my eye through the window between the dining room and the kitchen, and jerked his head backward in a summoning gesture.

When I could safely leave the kitchen for a moment, I went out to see what he wanted. "Good morning."

"Hey, Amy. How are you?"

"Fine, thanks. You?"

"I'm all right. Just wanted to let you know the guitar thing checked out," he said. "I mentioned to Ryan as we left the station last night that I've always wished I'd learned to play the piano. Then I asked if there was an instrument he'd like to learn. He said he'd hinted to his mom that he'd like a guitar for Christmas this year."

I smiled. "Thanks, Sheriff. I appreciate your detective work. How about I box up some doughnuts for you to take back to the station on the house?"

"I'll take a box of doughnuts, but I'm paying for them and my breakfast too." He shook his head. "The rest of the staff and I mooch too much free food off you as it is. You're going to keep on until you let your generosity run you out of business. Then the only place in this town to eat will be that pizza joint."

The door opened, and the sheriff made a comical grimace.

"Not that I have anything against good ol' pizza," he said. "I just don't want it to be Winter Garden's only option."

He needn't have worried about offending anyone—the newcomer was Belinda Carpenter's brother Adam, and I figured he didn't give a fig about the town's only other restaurant. In fact, I doubted he cared anything about this one either.

Since the early birds had already come and gone and it wasn't time for the lunch crowd yet, there were only a handful of patrons in the café.

Adam spoke to the room in general. "Howdy, folks."

"Hey there!" Scott said. "We have freshly-baked cinnamon sugar doughnuts, if you're interested."

The doughnuts had been such a hit that I'd already made more. The last batch was in the oven along with a tray of chocolate chip cookies.

"How is Belinda today, Adam?" I asked.

He sat at the counter with only one seat between him and Sheriff Billings, although there were several seats available. "The poor kid is broken-hearted, as I'm sure you can imagine." He was addressing the sheriff as much as or more than he was speaking to me. "We—our whole family, I mean—have managed to convince her she needs to leave Winter Garden and come home to Florida so she can have a strong support system in place."

I pretended not to notice that he wasn't really answering me as much as imparting this information to Sheriff Billings for whatever reason. Maybe he wanted to let the local authorities know Belinda was getting ready to leave town. After all, she might not have been eliminated as a suspect in her husband's death yet.

"I believe that's an excellent idea," I told Adam. "I thought she seemed frightened yesterday."

Sheriff Billings' eyes widened, but I ignored his look of warning.

"Frightened?" Adam echoed. "About what?"

"I don't know." I shrugged. "She didn't come right out and say she was scared, but she gave me the impression she was afraid that the person who sabotaged Devon's car might come after her too."

Scoffing, Adam said, "I'm still not convinced my brother-in-law's wreck wasn't an accident. I know everybody thinks those brake lines were purposefully cut, but there has to be a reasonable explanation. Devon was a great guy."

I opened my mouth to respond, but Sheriff Billings said, "Townspeople shouldn't be speculating about police investigations, especially when they lack all the pertinent information."

"That's right." Adam bobbed his head like a plastic dog toy on a dashboard. "No offense, but Winter Garden is full of busybodies."

His snide remark knocked my nose out of joint. "I wouldn't say that, Mr. Tate. I'd say Winter Garden is filled with people who care about each other's well-being."

"And I see the veracity in each of your observations." Sheriff Billings stood. "Scott, I'd appreciate it if you could ring me up when you have a minute."

"I'll meet you at the register, sir." Scott finished pouring a cup of coffee before he went to total the sheriff's order.

Adam turned and watched him go. As Sheriff Billings got into his car, Adam looked back at me. "You should keep your mouth shut about things that don't concern you."

"I was worried about Belinda, that's all."

"She's another one who needs to rein herself in." Adam shook his head. "Accidents happen and husbands die every day. Devon's unlucky day was last week."

"Do you really think that's all it was?" I asked. "Bad luck?"

He shrugged. "Why not? Makes as much sense as anything else." He narrowed his eyes. "Like I said, accidents happen every. Single. Day."

Although his tone implied a threat, I didn't feel frightened; I was angry. But before I could respond, Homer came in.

Scott, pouring coffee for an elderly couple and apparently unaware of the exchange that was taking place between Adam and me, greeted Homer effusively. "Good morning! I sure could use some wisdom this morning. What have you got for us?"

"My hero of the day is the American philosopher William James," Homer said. "Mr. James believed our greatest weapon against stress is our ability to choose one thought over another. So how can you think differently about any stresses in your life?"

Grinning broadly, Scott said, "That's the stuff."

Adam turned to leave.

"Mr. Tate, I hope you're not leaving on my account," Homer said.

"Nope." He cast a look in my direction as if I were a skunk that had just sprayed him. "I lost my appetite, that's all."

Adam stormed out of the café, and I tried unsuccessfully to relax my face into a smile for Homer.

"Amy, dear, Mr. James said, 'The art of being wise is the art of knowing what to overlook.' I don't know what transpired between you and Mr. Tate, but I seriously doubt it's worth ruining your day over."

"You're right." I took a deep breath. "You really do have a lot of wisdom to impart, Homer."

"Ah, it wasn't me—it was Mr. James," he said.

I was about to tell him I knew better when the timer on the oven went off. "I have to take care of some doughnuts and cookies, and then I'll get your sausage biscuit out."

He settled onto his usual stool. "No hurry."

I knew better than *that* too.

Chapter Nineteen

Scott had demonstrated a talent for decorating pastries in the past; so when he volunteered to help me work on the float cake this afternoon, I jumped at the chance. I asked if he'd mind decorating the second from the top tier to look like a Christmas-themed cake while I worked on the layer showcasing the burgers, hot dogs, chicken, and tacos. To provide continuity with my rosette borders, Scott decided to use the same tip to cover the entire cake with rows of green and red buttercream rosettes.

"That looks yummy," I said, as I tinted a ball of fondant blue and eyed the row of green rosettes Scott had piped along the bottom of the cake. "You'd kill me if I raked my finger through that, wouldn't you?"

"Nope."

I reached my hand out as if I might do what I'd threatened, and he squirted a dollop of icing onto my finger.

"Now you don't have to." He winked. "Diversion—the art of keeping animals and children happy."

I lowered my hand from my mouth after licking the icing off my gloved finger. "Are you calling me a puppy or a baby?"

"Neither." He laughed. "But, you know, if the paw fits, Puppy Girl..."

Squeaking in mock indignation, I again pretended I was going to mess up his work.

Naturally, that's the moment when Michelle strolled in. "Am I interrupting?"

"Not at all," I said quickly. "We have some extra help today. Isn't that great?"

"You are interrupting Amy trying to get at my icing." Scott held up the pastry bag. "Would you like a taste?"

"Indeed not." Michelle wrinkled her nose in disgust. "That's pure fat and sugar, and I care too much about my figure and my health to indulge."

"Aw, you need to live a little, Mrs. Hall," he said. "Life's too short to deny yourself buttercream."

Michelle merely gave Scott a stiff nod and went into the kitchen. I tossed the gloves I'd been wearing into the trash and put on a new pair before resuming my task of tinting the fondant.

Despite the Christmas music playing, I could hear Michelle in the kitchen. I tried to determine if she was banging things or simply making her usual level of noise. Her cool tone when she'd asked if she were interrupting assured me she thought Scott and I were up to no good and that she could hardly wait to inform Ryan of it. But the crack about caring about her health and physique—the underlying implication being that I did not—were typical Michelle remarks.

Oh, well, who cares what she thinks? I did. Still, I tried to tell myself I didn't.

When *The Twelve Days of Christmas* began to play, Scott sang along. He had a nice voice. I joined in along about the third day; and after putting her first batch of cookies in the oven, Michelle came into the dining room in time to harmonize on "five golden rings."

I stopped singing and froze when Mom and Aunt Bess stepped into the café. My eyes flew to Scott, who knew I wanted to surprise them with my float cake.

He never missed a beat. Putting aside his pastry bag, he stepped around the counter. "Two of my favorite ladies!" Spreading his arms, he enveloped them both in a hug, giving me the opportunity to sweep my cake onto the shelf beneath the counter.

"Mom, Aunt Bess, this is a nice surprise." I also went to give them hugs.

"Hi, I'm Michelle. It's nice to meet you both."

Mom had heard a few stories about Ryan's mom—some good and some not so good. She stepped forward and shook Michelle's hand. "Hi, I'm Jenna. It's a pleasure to meet you."

"Likewise," Michelle said. "And, of course, it's wonderful to meet the famous Aunt Bess. Ryan speaks highly of you both."

Mom didn't waste time getting straight to the point. "What are you all doing here after closing time?"

"I'm working on my piping skills," Scott said. "Amy can always use an extra hand with the baked goods, and I enjoy doing it."

"And she was kind enough to let me use her kitchen to make a huge batch of cookies." Ryan's mom apparently caught on quickly. "You'd think I'd learn to say no to people one of these days, but I keep finding myself in one predicament after another."

"What kind of cookies?" Aunt Bess asked.

"Sugar," Michelle answered. "Would you like me to save you some?"

"Oh, no. I'd never want anyone to go to any trouble on my account." Aunt Bess's downcast face belied her words.

Instead of saying, *since when,* I told her, "I've already set aside something special for you today. I was going to drop them off when we finished up here." I hurried to the kitchen and got the small box of doughnuts I'd prepared for Mom and Aunt Bess.

When I handed them to Aunt Bess, she seemed to be delighted with her treat. I turned to Mom. "Is anything wrong?" It wasn't like them to stop by unannounced.

"That's what we came to ask you. Aunt Bess and I were on our way home after a quick trip to the grocery store and saw cars in the parking lot. I was afraid something might be amiss here at the café."

"Not me. I wasn't afraid something was wrong." Aunt Bess grinned at Scott. "What scared me was the thought that you all were doing something fun here without me."

He scoffed. "How could anything possibly be fun without you?"

She beamed in my direction. "He does make an excellent point."

"He does." I smiled and shook my head.

"We'd better get home and put our groceries away now that we know everything is all right here," Mom said. "Michelle, it was a pleasure meeting you."

After Mom and Aunt Bess left, I blew out a breath. "That was close. I didn't know they were going anywhere today. Thank you both for helping me cover."

"Why don't you want them knowing about the important role you're playing in the town's parade?" Michelle asked.

"I want them to be surprised," I said. "And I also want them to be proud. Not only for my having a float in the Christmas parade but for what the float represents—my hard work, Nana's legacy, and the realization of a dream." I'd inherited the money to buy and renovate the café from my mom's mom.

Seeing that I was on the verge of tears, albeit happy ones, Scott did what he always did whenever he saw someone he cared about in an emotional situation—bear hug.

Scowling, Michelle returned to the kitchen. I could only imagine what she'd tell Ryan.

I went home, showered, changed clothes, had a sandwich, and fed Rory and Princess Eloise before going out again. Jackie had texted me earlier that Roger was bringing their dinner from a restaurant in Abingdon, so I planned to pay a visit to Belinda Carpenter. Not wanting to go to her home empty handed, but also not wanting to appear to be shoving Down South Café food in her face at every opportunity, I went by the local grocer's floral department and selected a tasteful arrangement.

"Amy, hi," Belinda said, upon opening her door. She scanned the area around me to ensure I was alone. I wondered if she was looking for Jackie or someone else. As she took the flowers, she invited me inside.

"These are beautiful." She placed the vase on a table in the living room. "Thank you."

"You're welcome." I jerked my head slightly in the direction of the window. "I was surprised to see a realtor's sign on your lawn."

"Yeah...although given the current state of the housing market in Winter Garden, I'm not anticipating a quick sale." She gestured toward the armchair. "Please have a seat. Would you like coffee?"

I declined.

Belinda perched on the edge of the sofa. "Why are you being so nice to me? You don't even know me. And from what I can understand, you didn't know Devon well either."

"You're right—I didn't. But I've been in a predicament similar to yours." I told her about my former boss being murdered and my finding her body. "If you're like I was then, you're under a lot of pressure. You don't know who to trust. You understand why you might be considered a suspect, and yet you still feel persecuted because of it. And you feel frightened. What if the killer comes after you?"

Nodding, she said, "I am scared...half to death."

"I also know it's hard to talk with the police." I spread my hands. "Ryan and Sheriff Billings are great—and the other members of the WGSD that I've met seem to be also—but I was always scared I'd say the wrong thing during interviews and end up implicating myself somehow."

"That's it." She leaned her elbows on her knees. "That's precisely how I feel when they come to talk with me."

I carefully weighed my words. What I wanted to say next could either open a floodgate or drop down an iron wall. "Do you think Devon's death had anything to do with the life he left behind in Florida?"

She stared at me in silence. I could clearly read the rapid-fire expressions as they flitted across her face: fear, suspicion, indecision.

Pressing on, I said, "Does what happened to him have anything to do with the name *Murphy*?"

Gasping, Belinda asked, "Who told you that name?"

"I came across it by accident when I was searching online for information about Devon."

"Why would you do that?" She got up and stalked over to the window. After a furtive glance outside, she turned and awaited my answer.

"One of my best friends is a suspect in your husband's murder," I said. "A search for a viable suspect other than Roger is what drove me to see what I could learn about Devon's past."

"But why is Roger a suspect? He and Devon got along great."

I shrugged. "The police always question everyone close to the victim. Plus, someone said they'd overheard them arguing."

"Over what?" she asked. "Jackie?"

"No. It had something to do with appliances." Because I was uneasy with the way Belinda was prowling around the living room peeping out the windows, I stood and walked toward her. "There was never anything between Devon and Jackie other than friendship."

"I know that now." Uttering a guttural cry, she said, "I wish I'd realized it before I got Devon killed."

Chapter Twenty

"Why do you think you got Devon killed?" I asked.

"Because I did." She was weeping then, and it was hard to understand what she was saying. "I...jealous."

"You were jealous of Jackie?"

Belinda nodded and composed herself enough to explain. "I knew Devon was talking with somebody and was trying to conceal that fact from me. Then I glimpsed a text from Jackie saying she'd send him a picture. When I asked Devon about it, he was really weird—he said he needed a photo of something he and Roger were working on. I wasn't buying that. I thought he and Jackie were having an affair."

"She was probably going to send him a snapshot of a necklace to see if it was what he was searching for," I murmured.

"I know that now! But I didn't then." She took a shuddering breath. "All I knew was that my husband was phoning and texting another woman and trying to keep it a secret from me. What would you have thought?"

"I'd have probably jumped to the same conclusion you did. What did Devon say when you asked him about it?"

Looking down at the floor, she said, "I didn't ask him. Instead, I confided in my best friend in Florida. Sheila was always more level-headed than I was, and I hoped she could tell me what I should do. But all I ended up doing was confirming our location."

"Confirming your location to whom?" I asked. "Why were you in hiding?"

Belinda closed her eyes and said nothing.

"When I ran across Devon's real name, it was in connection to a smuggling story on a newspaper's website." I took her gently by the arm and led her back to the sofa.

"Then you already know why we were hunkered down here in the middle of nowhere." She sank into the cushions.

"Are you in witness protection?" I hoped not because if they were, they had a terrible cover story.

"No. Devon didn't know his partner was involved in smuggling illegals into the country in the beginning. When he bought into the charter business, he believed it to be strictly for fishing and sightseeing." She gazed up at the ceiling. "He and I discussed it later, and the business probably was legitimate initially. But Rick—his partner, Richard D'Angelo—was always looking to make more money. We figured one of the smugglers came to him with a lucrative offer, and he started doing the smuggling on the side."

"And he hoped to keep Devon in the dark so he wouldn't have to share the profits," I said.

"Exactly. On the night their ship was raided, Devon had learned about the illegals on board just before their departure back to Florida. He knew there was no arguing about it until they got back, but Devon planned to tell Rick to either stop the smuggling or to buy him out."

The Christmas tree lights must've been on a timer because they came on and started blinking, casting an ethereal glow on the room. I wished I could turn them off because it made the situation even sadder somehow.

"Of course, they never got back to port that night," Belinda continued. "When the Coast Guard boarded the ship, Devon was able to slip into the water and swim out to a buoy. He clung to it for over an hour until he was rescued by the captain of a party barge. Once the barge docked, Devon called, asked me to pack up only what we needed, and to pick him up."

"So you came to Winter Garden to escape the authorities," I said.

"That's only half of it. Had we stayed in Florida, the people Rick was working for would've expected Devon to shoulder blame and, if necessary, go to prison for something he'd taken no part in." She sighed. "The authorities would've wanted to either prosecute Devon or give him a plea deal in exchange for information on the smuggling operation."

"But how could Devon provide information if he had no prior knowledge?" I wondered if maybe Devon's story to his wife about his not being involved had been a lie.

"He knew who booked the trip, and he knew who Rick had been working with to arrange everything," she said. "Poor Devon was between a rock and a hard place. Either he'd go to prison for something he didn't do or run the risk of being murdered for informing on the smugglers. We felt our only option was to change our names and move here."

Her story had more holes than Rory's favorite blanket. Why would they move to a place where they had family if they were trying to hide from everyone? "I thought one of Devon's relatives was a principal in the charter business?"

"Cyrus—yeah, he is. But, like Devon, he didn't realize what Rick was doing either."

"How did Cyrus avoid prosecution in the case?" I asked. "Or did he?"

"The feds gave him a hard time, and he thinks he's still being watched pretty closely. But it was his suggestion that we come here to Winter Garden and lie low for a while."

"If people from Florida knew where you were, why do you think you're responsible for Devon's death?" Was she blaming herself because she felt so guilty? "Anyone could've divulged your location."

Shaking her head, she said, "Only Cyrus and my closest family members knew where we'd gone. They'd have never give us up to Rick or the smugglers. But when I got jealous and called Sheila, I cost my husband his life."

"If Sheila was your best friend, why do you think she'd betray you?"

"For the money, I guess. I don't know." She plucked an accent pillow off the sofa and clutched it to her chest. "We heard from Adam not long after we left that the smugglers were going around offering to pay our friends for information."

"Still, don't you think the smugglers could've found Devon on their own? I imagine they're thorough and resourceful, not to mention desperate." I didn't say so to Belinda, but I wouldn't put it past Adam to betray Devon for money. He didn't strike me as the most loyal person in the world. "Have you spoken about any of this to the police?"

"No. I've been afraid to. What if they think I was involved with the smuggling and turn me over to the feds?"

"They wouldn't do that." I *hoped* they wouldn't do that. And I was fairly confident they *wouldn't* do that. "Why don't you let me call Ryan, and I'll stay here with you while you talk with him? The more he and Sheriff Billings know, the more they can help you."

Sniffling, she said, "All right."

Twenty minutes later, Belinda, Sheriff Billings, Ryan, and I were sitting at Belinda's kitchen table. I'd made coffee and was heating up the chicken casserole I'd brought over when Jackie and I had first visited Belinda upon hearing of Devon's death.

By the time Belinda finished telling them the same story she'd relayed to me, the casserole was hot. I removed it from the oven and spooned some onto plates for all of us.

"Belinda, you're obviously afraid for your life," Sheriff Billings said. "I'd like to put you into protective custody. Unfortunately, the Winter Garden Sheriff's Department doesn't have the manpower for that, so I'll have to reach out to county law enforcement to see if they'll lend us a hand."

"I don't want protection," Belinda said, poking her fork dejectedly into the food on the plate in front of her. "I deserve whatever happens to me."

"Now, you know that's not true." Sheriff Billings accepted the plate I handed to him. "Thank you, Amy."

"We'll have the agents involved in the smuggling case speak with Sheila to see if she did, in fact, tell someone you and Devon were in Winter Garden," Ryan said. "If she did tell someone—even innocently—her testimony could go a long way in helping us find Devon's killer."

I set a plate in front of Ryan and took one for myself before sitting down. "When would the county be able to start the protective custody for Belinda?"

"That's hard to say." Sheriff Billings sipped his coffee. "It will take at least a day or two to get the process started. In the meantime, I'd suggest you stay home and be extremely careful about who you open your door to, Belinda."

"I'm not comfortable having Belinda stay here alone," I said. "I have plenty of room at my place."

I saw Ryan and Sheriff Billings exchange glances before Ryan said, "Before I forget, I have something in the car I need to show you, Amy."

"Right now?" *Of course, right now. I'm the one who invented something in the car to mean I need to talk with you privately immediately.*

"Please." He wiped his mouth, put down his napkin, and scooted his chair back.

I was already preparing my defense in my head as we walked out Belinda's door.

"I am not out of my mind," I said as soon as we got out onto the porch.

"I didn't say you were." He inclined his head. "But you know what they say about the shoe..."

"Marilyn Monroe said something about the right pair changing your life, but I've got a feeling that's not the quote you're referencing."

"Amy, you cannot invite this woman into your home. You don't even know her."

"I realize that, but she's afraid for her life." I took his arm. "Before you and the sheriff got here, she was prowling around peeping out the windows and jumping at every sound she heard."

"And yet that could be an act." He turned and put his arms around me. "I love how sensitive you are, but Belinda could be covering for the fact that she's the one who killed her husband."

"I don't think so," I said. "I believe she's devastated over Devon's death."

"Even if she is, if you take her into your home, you could be putting yourself and even your mom and Aunt Bess in danger." He hugged me tighter. "If Devon's killer is still here, then he or she is willing to do whatever is necessary to keep any witnesses from talking."

"But what can we *do*?" I felt that I couldn't turn my back on this woman who was so frightened of being murdered in her own home. But Ryan was right—I couldn't put Mom and Aunt Bess in danger either.

"I don't know." He kissed the top of my head. "The sheriff will come up with something."

And Sheriff Billings did have an idea. He took Belinda into custody. He could hold her for ninety-six hours without charging her for a crime. We—or, rather, they—had four days to find Devon's killer.

Chapter Twenty-One

On Thursday morning, Dilly and Walter were discussing the news about a person of interest being held in Devon's murder investigation when they came in.

Playing dumb, I asked, "What's going on?"

"Haven't you seen today's newspaper?" Dilly asked.

"No." Truth be told, I seldom looked at a physical copy of the Winter Garden News. These days, I was more apt to check the news online.

"The story is on the front page," Walter said.

Dilly was too excited to let Walter be the one to tell me. "Although the article doesn't say who's being held, we're convinced Devon's murder will be solved soon."

"I'm glad his poor wife will get some closure before Christmas." Walter shook his head. "Not much consolation in that, I know, but—"

"I believe she's the one they're holding," Dilly interjected.

"Now, sweet darling, the paper said no charges have been filed against this person of interest yet. Even if it is Belinda who's being held, that's no reason to jump to the conclusion that the woman is guilty."

Dilly rolled her eyes. "You're such a gentleman. You don't want to believe a woman is capable of such treachery."

It was at that moment that Bryson Neal came into the café. "What's this about treachery?" He grinned. "I feel as if I've walked in on a Shakespearean production. I don't often hear that word being thrown around."

"I merely detest the thought of anyone murdering a loved one," Walter said. "I know it happens, but I despise it. Devon appeared to be such a fine young man. I suppose I was still clinging to the hope that his death was the result of a horrible accident."

"Wait—" Bryson sank onto a stool at the counter. "There's been an arrest in Devon Carpenter's murder?"

"No," Walter said, emphatically. "The Winter Garden News reports that a person of interest is being held for questioning. Nothing was mentioned about an arrest being made at this time."

"Were you well acquainted with the couple?" I asked Bryson.

"Um...not really. I mean, I met them once through a mutual friend at a tailgating party. Granted, I didn't know them well, but they seemed to be happy," he said. "I suppose we only see what people want us to believe about their lives. It's hard to imagine what secrets could be lurking in someone's home."

"That's true, but we're all jumping to conclusions," Walter said. "Nobody has been charged with anything. And even if Belinda Carpenter is being held in police custody, it could simply mean she's a material witness in the case."

"Walter has a point," Scott said, bringing the coffee pot to fill everyone's cups. "The sheriff could be on a fishing expedition."

While I was in the kitchen preparing breakfast for Dilly, Walter, and Bryson, I used my headset to call Mom. Aunt Bess answered.

"Good morning, Aunt Bess. You're up early. Is Mom around?"

"She's in the shower."

"Well, I was calling to ask if you'd save today's Winter Garden News for me," I said.

"Who died?"

"Nobody." I suppressed a giggle. "No need to update your *People I've Outlived* board as far as I know. I'm just interested in an article Dilly was telling me about."

"Dilly Boyd knows something I don't?" She huffed. "I doubt that."

And I knew Aunt Bess well enough to know she'd barely had the chance to rub the sleep out of her eyes this early in the morning.

"Hold on," she demanded.

I tried to tell her it was all right, that I'd see her and Mom later today, but she'd left me hanging. While I waited for her to return, I flipped my pancakes.

"It says here on the front page that Sheriff Billings is holding a person of interest in the Devon Carpenter murder investigation," Aunt Bess's voice practically shouted. "Did you know about this and not tell me?"

I answered carefully so I wasn't lying to Aunt Bess. I mean, I knew Sheriff Billings had taken Belinda into protective custody, but I had no idea the newspaper's longtime editor Ms. Peggy had learned about it and put it on the front page of the *Winter Garden News.*

"What do you think?" I asked her. "You could've knocked me over with a feather when Dilly came in saying that story was on the front page of the newspaper. That's why I called to have you and Mom hold onto it for me—I want to read that article this evening."

"Well, I'm reading it right now. Do you want me to tell you what it says?"

"As much as I appreciate the offer, I can't accept because I'm too busy, Aunt Bess. The breakfast rush is about to hit. I'll look at it later."

After ending the call, I wondered who leaked the information to Ms. Peggy. Had someone seen the sheriff leaving the Carpenter house with Belinda? Had the sheriff given Ms. Peggy the information to draw out the killer? If the article had been run in an attempt to set tongues to wagging, it had certainly worked. Our patrons were speculating about the Devon Carpenter murder all day long.

Following the lunch rush, I called Ryan and asked him how Ms. Peggy learned that a person of interest had been detained in conjunction with Devon's murder investigation.

"There was a leak in the Sheriff's Department," he said.

"Oh, no! Do you know who leaked it?"

"Yep. The sheriff."

"He did?" I asked. "Why?"

"To advance the investigation. In fact, Sheriff Billings wrote the article himself so it would be worded exactly as he wanted it." He chuckled. "He's awfully proud of his journalism. Have you seen it yet?"

"I haven't, but I'll look at it later at the big house. Aunt Bess is keeping the newspaper for me," I said. "She was perturbed when she thought I had inside information and didn't tell her before it found its way to Ms. Peggy's desk."

"Speaking of perturbed people, Mom didn't care for Scott's overly friendly behavior toward you yesterday."

I laughed. "She didn't try to hide that fact from me. I knew she thought he and I were up to something."

"You *were*! I heard about how well he helped you hide your float cake from Aunt Bess and Jenna. If you think Aunt Bess is miffed over having to find out what's going on in the jail from the newspaper, imagine how ticked she'll be when she sees your float for the first time there among the huddled masses."

It dawned on me Ryan was right. She *would* be upset. I'd wanted to surprise her and Mom, but I didn't want them to feel excluded. "Do you think I should invite them to the café tomorrow evening to see the assembled cake before the parade on Saturday?"

"Absolutely."

"I'm glad you pointed out the error of my ways," I said. "I thought I was doing something fun—but I can still surprise them tomorrow at the café. By the way, today's special was chicken and dumplings, but they're going fast. I'll make cheeseburgers, hot dogs, and fries to bring to the police station after work for you, the sheriff, and Belinda."

"That sounds great, but you know we have food prepared for our prisoners, right?"

"Yes." I was stubborn. But jail food couldn't compete with *my* food—could it? "Do you have a preference for dessert?"

"Surprise me. You like surprises."

Smart aleck.

When Michelle arrived that afternoon, I was packing up dinner for the station and Belinda. I was including a care package for Belinda.

"I have to run these boxes over to the Sheriff's Department," I said. "Would you like to go?"

"Shouldn't you be working on the cake?"

"I will. This won't take long." I used my trump card. "I know Ryan would love to see you." Okay, it might've been a stretch, but it worked.

At the station, Ryan seemed glad not only to see his mom but to see the two of us together. I was happy he had a good relationship with Mom, and I imagined he wanted me and his mom to get along well. I wanted that too.

"We've brought food." I indicated the smaller box. "And I've brought a care package for Belinda." I opened the box because I knew that if it were any other visitor and any other prisoner—even though Belinda was here for her own safety—the box's contents would need to be approved.

Michelle eased closer to observe what was in the box. There were a couple of magazines, three novels (because I didn't know what genre Belinda would prefer), a soft blanket, a washcloth and towel, and a bar of finely milled lavender-scented soap.

Ryan grinned at me. "This is a jail, not the Ritz. We have blankets, towels, and books, you know."

"I'm only trying to be nice."

He kissed the tip of my nose, handed me the box, and said, "Take it on back."

"Thank you." I caught a glimpse of Michelle as I went back to the holding cells. She had a smile more mysterious than that of the Mona Lisa on her face. I wondered what it meant.

"Amy, hi!" Belinda stood and moved closer when I neared her cell.

A matron hovered but wasn't overly intrusive.

"I brought you a care package." I handed it to her through the bars. "If you need anything else, please have Ryan let me know."

"I will, thank you." She took the box back over to her cot and opened it up.

I waited as she *oohed* and *aahed* over the contents.

Picking up one of the novels, she said, "I've been wanting to read this one."

"Good. I'm glad I chose well."

"I appreciate everything you've done for me." She walked back over to the door of her cell. "You don't even know me, and yet you've treated me better than my own family has. Adam came to see me for about fifteen minutes today; and the whole time he was here, he kept telling me to keep my mouth shut." She lowered her head. "He did say he'd try to find me an attorney, but I told him I didn't need one—that I was being held as a witness, not a suspect. That agitated him even more."

"People react differently in a crisis," I said. "Maybe Adam is helping in the only way he knows how—by trying to protect you and get you out of here."

But I couldn't help wondering if that was what he was actually doing or if he was sweating bullets over what his sister might divulge about the smuggling operation.

Chapter Twenty-Two

After work, I went to visit Mom and Aunt Bess.

Aunt Bess hurried into the kitchen to get the newspaper. "I saved this for you. I also high-lighted what I felt were the most important parts."

I took the folded newspaper she thrust at me. The entire article was bathed in yellow ink. *Where in the world did Aunt Bess get a highlighter?* "Thanks."

The article said, in part: *The Winter Garden Sheriff's Department is holding a person of interest in the Devon Carpenter murder investigation. No charges have been formally filed, and it is hoped this individual might be able to shed light not only on the*

Carpenter murder but also on crimes originating in the state of Florida.

Aunt Bess had penned a note in the margin here saying, *What happened in Florida? Investigate!*

I had to bite my tongue from saying Sheriff Billings did a good job with the piece—the byline was that of Ms. Peggy. But the sheriff had certainly drawn a line in the sand with the article. If Devon's killer were still here in Winter Garden and hadn't been attempting to murder Belinda, he—or she—would be gunning for her now. And unless Sheriff Billings had the killer in custody within the next three days, Belinda would be in serious jeopardy. I prayed the sheriff knew what he was doing.

"Well, Angels," Mom said, coming into the living room and sitting on the sofa beside Aunt Bess. "Have we any new developments in the case?"

"Mark my words—it's one of those cousins who resented the fact that Devon's aunt left him that house," Aunt Bess said.

"Actually—" I started to tell them I thought Devon *bought* the house, but that wasn't a fact I wanted to debate at the moment. Instead, I said, "I have a surprise for you two. Could you come to the café tomorrow after closing?"

Aunt Bess leaned forward and rubbed her hands together. "Are we setting a trap for Devon Carpenter's killer? Would you like for me to be the bait?"

"No!"

Mom and I spoke the word simultaneously.

"I'm not setting a trap for anyone," I said, wondering what programs Aunt Bess had been watching on TV, "but that's all I'm telling you. You'll have to wait and see. Otherwise, it wouldn't be a surprise."

"I don't like surprises," she grumbled. "I'm old. What if I die in my sleep tonight?"

"If you die in your sleep, you won't know what you've missed because you'll be so delighted by heaven," Mom said.

"Oh, you'd like for me to be left out of the surprise. Is that what you're saying, Jenna?"

Rolling her eyes, Mom replied, "No, Aunt Bess. I'd never want you to be left out of anything."

"Well, that's good. Because—by crackies—I don't intend to miss a trick."

On Friday morning, I awoke before the alarm went off and felt optimistic. This was going to be a good day. I was going to assemble the cake, show it to Mom and Aunt Bess, prepare the Bug for the parade, and help Michelle finish up the cookies. And all that was to follow a full day's work at the café. But I didn't dread it—I was excited about it.

I was contemplating how the day would unfold when Princess Eloise pounced onto the center of my chest. That was odd. Where was Rory? It was usually he who bounded into my room to demand food and attention.

After stroking Princess Eloise under the chin and setting her aside, I sat up and called to Rory. No bark or clicking of approaching paws.

I got out of bed, slid my feet into my slippers, and headed down the hall. I called to and looked for Rory as I walked. A quick search of the house proved futile, so I thought he must've gone out through the doggie door into the backyard. Stepping out onto the back porch, I gasped when I saw my sweet dog playing tug-of-war with Adam Tate through the fence. Thank goodness I'd put a padlock on the gate.

"Rory, come!"

He ignored me and refused to give up on the game.

I redirected my attention to Adam. "What are you doing here?"

"I wanted to talk with you," he said. "But in private—not at the café."

If he was expecting me to invite him into my house, he was sorely mistaken. "Why not at the café? We can have a private conversation there."

"I don't want to risk our being overheard. It's about Belinda."

Glad as I was that my pajamas were flannel, I still didn't relish being outdoors within eyesight of a creepy stranger in my pjs. "Would you please let go of that toy so Rory will come in?"

"It's not a toy—it's my scarf." As he spoke, he released it, and Rory ran to me with his prize.

Taking the scarf from the plucky pup, I said, "I'll go in and change and meet you out front."

"Great. Thanks."

I went inside, got dressed, and put on my coat. I turned on the light and stepped out onto the porch.

Adam was sitting on one of my white wicker rockers. "It's getting colder. Winter Garden might wind up with a white Christmas."

"We'll see." I handed him his scarf and remained standing. "What was so important that you had to come to my home before daylight?"

"Belinda didn't kill Devon," he said.

"Have you made your case to the police?"

He shook his head. "What's the use? You think they're just gonna take my word for it?"

"They might. And they're in a much better position to assist you than I am." I crossed my arms. "How could I possibly help?"

"You can tell me what they've got on her." He stood. "I'll know what to do if I know what evidence they have."

"To my knowledge, Belinda hasn't been charged with a crime," I said. "And even if she had, I wouldn't know anything about the evidence in the case."

Adam took a step toward me. "Your boyfriend is one of the main investigators in the case. You're bound to know *something*."

My phone was in my pocket with the sheriff's office number ready to be dialed at the touch of a button. I stood my ground and refused to be intimidated. "I *know* absolutely nothing about Devon's murder investigation. I *believe* Belinda is innocent, that she's heartbroken over the loss of her husband, that she fears for her life, and that she wishes her brother would be more supportive."

"I *am* supporting her!"

At Adam's raised voice, Rory began barking.

"Please leave," I said calmly. "And don't come back to my home uninvited again."

Adam stared at me long enough to make me think he might not leave. Then he muttered a curse and jumped off the porch.

I quickly went back inside and locked the door. As I fed the pets, I wondered how Adam had found my home. Had he done an internet search? Had he followed me? Had he simply been driving along, recognized my car, and thought he should drop in for a pre-sunrise visit? No matter how he'd found me, I wasn't happy about it. And I knew Ryan wouldn't be either.

Ryan was at the café waiting for me when I got there.

I tried to hide my smile—not wanting him to know how delighted I was to see him—but I couldn't. "You didn't have to do this."

"I wanted to. When you called and said that creep was waiting outside your house when you got up this morning, there was no way I was going to have you opening up by yourself."

Kissing him hello, I said, "But you're not even on duty yet." He looked magnificent in jeans, a blue sweater, and a black jacket, but I kept that to myself.

"I'm not here in a judicial capacity."

"I could whip you up something special for breakfast." I unlocked the café, and we went inside.

"Like what?" He flipped on the light switch.

"Whatever you'd like—bacon and eggs, Belgian waffles, blueberry pancakes."

"How about chocolate chip pancakes?" he asked.

I nodded. "I'm on it. Just let me get the coffee pots percolating."

"I can handle that," Jackie said.

"Jackie!" I hugged her.

"Yeah, yeah, I'm back to the land of the living." She looked at Ryan. "What're you doing here so early? I thought you had the late shift this week."

"I do." He looked at me, giving me the option to tell Jackie what had happened or not.

I explained that I'd discovered Adam Tate outside my house this morning—actually, outside the fenced backyard—playing tug-of-war with Rory.

"Is Rory all right?" she asked.

"He's fine. He wasn't keen on having to give up Adam's scarf, but I traded him a dental bone."

"Why in the world was he at your house playing with your dog before daylight?" Jackie asked. "That's super creepy."

"He said he wanted to talk with me privately—was afraid we'd be overheard here."

She looked around the café and spread her arms. "Yeah, this place is bustling at this time of day."

"Has Roger been getting any weird visits or calls from Adam?" Ryan asked.

"Not Adam, but Devon's cousin, Chris, came to see Roger on a job site yesterday morning," she said.

"What did he want?" I asked, as I walked into the kitchen to get started on Ryan's pancakes.

"A job. He said he'd been considering going to Florida and working on the charter boat with Adam, but—and this is a direct quote according to Roger—'that's just not my scene.' Besides that, he doesn't know Adam well enough to trust him."

"He said that?" I took my mixing bowl to the window where I could see and talk with Jackie and Ryan as I worked.

"He did," Jackie said. "Roger says he asked him, 'What if that dude and his sister knocked off my cousin?'"

"What did Roger tell him about the job?" Ryan asked.

"He said business is slow this time of year and to check back with him the first week in January." She grinned. "He's very diplomatic."

"Did Chris seem angry at Roger's answer?" Ryan took a couple of packets of sugar and one of creamer in anticipation of the coffee being almost ready. Its comforting aroma was already filling the café.

"No," she said. "He thanked Roger and said he hopes to work with him after the first of the year. Roger thinks maybe the rats are trying to desert a sinking ship."

Ryan nodded. "With luck, they're about to turn on each other and tell us who killed Devon Carpenter."

Chapter Twenty-Three

Homer was bubbling over with contagious enthusiasm when he came into the café at his usual time.

"You seem to have even more spring in your step than usual today, Guru Guy," Scott said.

As Homer took a seat on his regular stool, Jackie poured him a coffee.

"I'm happy to see you back at work, young lady," he said. "I trust you're well?"

"I am." She placed the cup in front of him. "I was bored to tears staying at home watching television and taking medicine every six hours."

"Who's your hero today?" I asked.

"The entrepreneur Jim Rohn, who I believe has been my hero more than once over the years. Mr. Rohn once said that happiness isn't something you postpone for the future—it's something you design for the present." He smiled as he stirred sugar into his coffee. "Have I told you how honored and pleased I am to hand out cookies for you during the parade tomorrow?"

"You have," I said. "Have I told you how glad we are to have your help?"

"Yes, ma'am. You make me feel like a true member of the Down South family."

"You are!"

Jackie, Scott, and I spoke at once.

"I'll be on the opposite side of the road from you," Scott told Homer. "Jackie, Luis, and Oscar are going to hold down the fort here, so I can give out cookies too."

Homer nodded. "You know, it would be optimal to have four distributors—two on either side of the car. I could possibly recruit someone."

"I'm going to see if Donna and her children would be interested." I knew I should've asked them long before now, but it had been a tough week. Besides, if push came to shove, two people handing out cookies should be enough. Parades move slowly.

Still, I made a mental note to call Donna as soon as I'd served Homer his sausage biscuit.

While I was in the kitchen preparing said biscuit, Adam Tate came into the café and sat beside Homer. I knew this because over the Christmas music and the sound of the few diners in the café, I heard Jackie's raised voice.

"What's up with you, Adam? Did you get hungry while you were lurking in the bushes waiting for my cousin to come outside?"

I hurried out of the kitchen with Homer's sausage biscuit on a plate hoping to diffuse the situation. Jackie was more protective than a Doberman Pinscher and twice as fierce.

After placing Homer's food in front of him, I went over and put a hand on Jackie's arm.

Before I could speak, Adam said, "I'm really ashamed of how I behaved this morning. I was so upset over my sister being taken into police custody that I completely lost it."

"What did you do?" Scott asked, stepping closer to me. He hadn't been at work yet when Ryan, Jackie, and I were discussing the morning's events.

Luis came in from the kitchen and stood nearby as well. I appreciated my crew closing ranks, but I felt perfectly safe here in the café. I'd have loved to have had them on hand this morning, though.

Playing devil's advocate, Homer said, "Mr. Rohn—a man wiser than I—once said that effective communication is twenty percent what you know and eighty percent how you feel about what you know. It appears to me that Adam's concern for Belinda swapped those numbers and hampered his attempt at expressing himself."

"I don't care how upset a man is," Jackie said. "He doesn't have the right to creep around a woman's home before daylight."

"Sorry," Homer said to Adam. "She's got you there. You really botched whatever it was you were trying to do."

"I know I messed up," Adam said, "and I sincerely apologize. If you don't want to serve me, I understand."

"Of course, we want to serve you," I said, ignoring the daggers shooting from Jackie's eyes. "What would you like?"

"Scrambled eggs and hash browns would be awfully good."

"Coming right up." I returned to the kitchen. That call to Donna would have to wait a few minutes longer.

Within two minutes, Jackie was storming into the kitchen to stand beside me at the grill. "That guy has a lot of nerve. He's trying to find out from Scott if the police have mentioned what evidence they have on Belinda."

"Why? Do you think he knows Scott's sister is the department's crime scene tech?"

"I don't think so," she said. "I believe he thinks small-town officers are such hayseeds that they discuss their cases at the local café. It's insulting! Not even Andy Taylor and Barney Fife would do such a thing—unless it was some sort of setup."

"I know." I transferred Adam's eggs to a plate. "But please settle down. Getting this worked up can't be good for you on your first day back at work."

"It's not going to be good for Adam Tate either if he doesn't keep his big mouth shut."

It wasn't until after Homer had finished his sausage biscuit and left that I was able to phone Donna.

"Hi, Amy!" Donna always sounded as if she were delighted to hear from me. "You sound funny—is everything all right?"

"Everything is great. I'm on my headset, so that's probably the reason I sound strange."

"Gotcha. What's up? Need me to pull an emergency shift?" she asked.

"Nothing like that. I just wondered if maybe your kids would like to walk along beside my car—which is serving as a float with a huge dummy cake on top—and hand out cookies to onlookers at the parade on Saturday."

"Oh, darn. I wish I'd known sooner, but they left this morning going to Elizabethton to spend the weekend with their grandparents." She sighed. "Would you like me to help?"

"No way," I said. "Enjoy spending some quiet time with your husband. I've got it covered—I just thought it might be a fun thing for them to do."

"I know they'd have loved every second of it. In fact, I'm not going to tell them they missed out."

"Good thinking. Thank you, Donna. I'll talk with you soon!" As I ended the call, I berated myself for not calling her sooner. It would've been fun for the kids, and I'd have had two extra pairs of hands. Oh, well, Homer and Scott were up to the task. And, if not, maybe I could talk Mom into driving the Beetle so I could help hand out cookies.

"Hi, folks!"

Frowning, I went to peep through the window into the dining room. Although that booming voice sounded familiar, I couldn't place it until I spotted Bryson Neal.

"Are you all as excited about tomorrow as I am?" he asked.

"We're pretty pumped," Scott said.

Adam looked up from his plate. "What's tomorrow?"

"Why, it's the Christmas parade," Bryson said. "And these fine people have a float that's going to be the talk of the town. You must not be from around here."

"I'm not." Adam stood and walked to the register. "Must be nice not to have anything more to worry about than a parade."

Scott met him at the register and rang up his order.

Bryson walked over there too. "What's got you so down?"

Adam shook his head. "You wouldn't understand."

"Try me. I'm the town manager. Maybe there's something I could help you with."

"Can you get my sister released from jail?" Adam asked.

Shrugging, Bryson said, "Maybe. Depends on what she's done."

"She hasn't done anything. Her name is Belinda Carpenter, and she's being held without any justification."

"I'm sorry to hear that. Let's you and I go over to the Sheriff's Department and find out what's going on." He nodded toward Scott and me. "I'm sorry to run out like this, but it sounds as if this matter needs my immediate attention."

As Bryson and Adam left the café together, Jackie turned to me. "Should we call the Sheriff's Department and warn them?"

"The number is already dialed," I said.

Chapter Twenty-Four

I called Ryan to let him know Bryson Neal and Adam Tate were on their way over to the Sheriff's Department.

"I don't know what Bryson hopes to accomplish," I told him, "but I thought you should be forewarned."

"Thanks for calling, sweetheart. I'll go let Sheriff Billings know."

After speaking with Ryan, I stepped into the dining room and saw that the café was currently devoid of customers. Knowing that would quickly change, I asked Scott, Jackie, and Luis, "What do you think Bryson hopes to accomplish by taking Adam to talk with Sheriff Billings?"

Scott leaned against the counter. "I think it's politics. The guy has only been in office for a month, and he wants to either make a good impression or take some sort of stand."

"He could want the town to know he's a caring person and that he's concerned about its citizens," Luis said.

"You're both wrong." Jackie started making a fresh pot of decaf. "That guy is nosy, and he's dying to know what's going on in Devon's murder investigation."

Chris Carpenter came in and apparently overheard Jackie's answer. "I hate to interrupt, but I'm nosy too. Who's trying to find out about Devon's case?"

"Bryson Neal, the town manager," I said. "He and Adam Tate left a few minutes ago. Bryson said they were going to see the sheriff about why he's holding Belinda."

"I'm not sure I'd trust either of those guys," Chris said. "One's a politician, and the other just strikes me as sketchy."

"Were you and Devon close?" I handed Chris a menu.

"About as close as two cousins who live five states away from each other could be, I reckon." He took the menu, opened it, and laid it flat on the counter. "We saw Devon for a week or two every summer. I always looked forward to that. We'd get to do stuff we didn't usually do when Devon was in town."

"Like what?" Jackie asked.

"We'd go to whatever carnival was in town or nearby, go to the water park, go get ice cream..." He shrugged. "Momma always felt sorry for Devon. She said his daddy was no-account and that his momma had trouble making ends meet."

"Is that why she left him the property?" I asked the question, even though Belinda had said Devon had bought the house while Chris had previously said his mom had left it to Devon. I wanted to see which story I'd get from Chris this time.

"Nah, we didn't have much either. Just because we were doing better than Devon and them didn't mean we were rich," Chris said. "When I said our momma left that property to Devon, it was a lie. He bought that place off me when he came up here from Florida. It was Daddy's old hunting cabin. I wasn't using it, and Devon needed it. I told him he and Belinda could live there for as long as they wanted, but he wouldn't hear of it. Said he wasn't a freeloader."

"How do you feel about Belinda?" Jackie asked.

"I don't trust her any more than I do her brother." He looked up from the menu. "Could I get a hot dog, tater tots, and a chocolate milk shake?"

"Coming right up." I headed to the kitchen as the parking lot started to fill for the lunch rush.

After closing, Scott and I were cleaning the windows.

I looked around to ensure no one else could hear us before asking, "How's Ivy?"

"Morning sickness is totally kicking her butt," he said softly. "Right now, it's more like all-day sickness. But I've been reading up, and hopefully, the sickness will be gone by the second trimester."

I sat back on my heels and looked up at him. "You are the greatest brother in the world."

"Face it, Amy-Girl. I'm pretty fantastic period."

Laughing, I said, "Yes, you are."

Ryan and Michelle came into the café together.

"This is a nice surprise," I said.

"How did the meeting go between Bryson Neal and Sheriff Billings, buddy?" Scott asked. "Are we talking *Law and Order* or *People's Court*?"

Ryan scrunched up his face. "More like *Let's Make a Deal*, but Sheriff Billings wouldn't play. Poor Bryson Neal isn't much of a town manager. I expected him to come into the station with guns blazing—figuratively speaking—and demand that the sheriff either charge Belinda Carpenter or let her go. Instead, he asked Sheriff Billings if he could speak with Belinda and Adam alone."

"Is he an attorney too?" Michelle asked.

"He is not, Mom. That's why the sheriff told him he could only conduct his meeting in the presence of an officer. They went back, Bryson asked Belinda if she was being treated well, she said she was, and then Bryson and Adam left."

"Gee, what a doormat," Scott said. "He's not getting my vote."

"Is he running for something?" I asked.

"Not that I know of. But if he were, I'd vote for the other candidate." Scott finished the window he was working on. Then, with a wide grin, he went and held open the door. "I see trouble, and she's headed this way!"

Aunt Bess grinned all over her face. "You know it, handsome." She kissed his cheek. "If I was twenty years younger, this one wouldn't be single."

Michelle looked at me. "It appears Scott is practically a member of the family."

"You bet he is," Aunt Bess said. "Are you and Ryan here to see the surprise too?"

"We sure are," Ryan said. "I can hardly wait."

Ryan, of course, knew about the cake, but this was the first time any of us were seeing it assembled.

"Scott, would you give me a hand?" I asked.

He applauded.

I shook my head.

"Oh...with the c—*surprise*," he said.

"What a wit you have," Aunt Bess told Scott. "I should probably help you two as well."

"You'll stay right here with me," Mom said, gently taking Aunt Bess's arm and keeping her from following Scott and me.

Aunt Bess folded her arms across her ample chest. "You're just afraid I'll see the surprise first."

"That's exactly what I'm afraid of."

In the kitchen, Scott and I assembled the tiers. I clasped my hand over my mouth. The cake looked even better than I'd hoped it would.

"You did an awesome job," Scott said.

"*We* did an awesome job." I blinked back tears. "They're gonna freak!"

"Yeah, they are." He moved to the far end of the cake board so he could back out the kitchen door into the dining room. "Get your end and let's go make their mouths drop open."

"Everybody, turn around until I say you can look!" I called.

I got my end, and Scott and I gingerly carried the cake into the dining room and sat it on a table in the center of the room.

"All right," I said. "See what you think."

They all turned. Michelle, who'd been watching the cake progress throughout the week, merely smiled.

"Oh, my gosh!" Mom exclaimed, hurrying over to get a better look.

Ryan laughed. "That's amazing!"

"That's too pretty to eat," Aunt Bess said.

"It's a good thing you think this cake is too pretty to eat," I said to Aunt Bess. "The layers are made of Styrofoam."

She frowned. "Why the dickens would you spend all of this time on a cake you can't eat?"

"Because I'm putting it on top of the Bug and driving it down the road in tomorrow's Christmas parade," I said.

Gasping, Aunt Bess said, "I call shotgun!" She quickly looked at Mom. "You can't because I've already called it."

Mom chuckled. "You can ride shotgun."

Gayle Leeson

"Yes, indeed, I can." Aunt Bess waved her fists in the air. "I'd drive if Amy would let me."

"I'm not going to let you," I said. "Michelle had the great idea of handing out cookies as further promotion for the café. She's been here baking every evening."

Scott went into the kitchen and brought out a box filled with bagged and tagged mini cookies. "Homer and I are handing these out."

"Yeah, Homer thought it would be better if there was a team of four," I said, "but I believe two will be plenty."

"I can help hand out cookies," Mom said. "I bet Clark would be game for it too. I'll call and ask him when we get home."

"What should I wear?" Aunt Bess asked.

I went to the merchandise rack behind the cash register and got some t-shirts. "How about a *Down South Café* t-shirt?" I handed two to Mom—one for her and one for Clark—and one to Aunt Bess.

Aunt Bess handed hers back. "No, thanks. You all wear what you want to. But if I'm being in a parade with the whole town turning out to see me, I'm gonna give them something to see."

"Atta girl!" Scott laughed. "Ah, if I was twenty years older, you wouldn't be single, Aunt Bess."

Chapter Twenty-Five

Walter and Dilly came in excited about the parade on Saturday morning.

"The car looks fantastic!" Dilly exclaimed.

Thanks to Scott and Luis, not only was the cake on the roof, but it had been draped with *Down South Café* banners on each side.

"We're going to have the perfect weather," Walter said. "Sunny and cool, but not so cold that our noses will run while we're watching the parade."

"Do you know anything about Belinda?" Dilly asked. "The newspaper said she hadn't been charged, but I haven't heard whether or not Sheriff Billings is still holding her."

As she was speaking, Chris Carpenter came into the café. "I heard you talking about Belinda." He rubbed his nose with the back of his hand. "I wish the sheriff would go ahead and charge her with accessory to murder because, in my opinion, that's what she is."

"Really?" Dilly patted the chair beside her. "Tell us more."

Chris took the seat. "Belinda told me and her brother, Adam, that she called her best friend, Sheila, in Florida to talk about Devon. She thought Devon was running around with another girl."

Jackie stiffened. "I'm going to do some extra prep work. We're going to be slammed when you and Scott leave."

"All right." Loudly enough so Jackie could hear, I added, "Belinda told me that as well, and I know her fears were completely unfounded."

"I know it too," Chris said. "Devon was as loyal as the day is long. But her friend, Sheila, is Devon's old partner's girlfriend now, and Uncle Cyrus told me Ricky was awfully worried about what Devon might say to the feds."

"Oh, my gosh." I lifted my hand slowly to my chest. "Do you think Ricky thought Devon was talking with the *feds* rather than to another woman?"

"That's exactly what I think." He waved to Scott as he walked by. "Hey, could I please get a cup of coffee?"

"Sure, man."

"I'm sorry," I said. "I should've offered. I got too engrossed in our conversation."

"It's all right," Scott said. "I've got it."

"Chris, did Ricky know where Devon was all along?" I asked.

"He at least suspected." Chris shrugged. "Ricky has family in Virginia too, so he, Devon, and Uncle Cyrus used to talk about things they'd done around here and Ricky's hometown. Anyway, Uncle Cyrus told Devon to watch his back because he thought Ricky had sent somebody around to keep an eye on him."

I got goosebumps. "Do you know who it was?"

Chris shook his head. "No idea. I was never in Florida, so I didn't meet Ricky or any of his crew. And, of course, his family wasn't from this part of Virginia. They were from Roanoke or somewhere up north."

My goosebumps got goosebumps. Devon was killed because Belinda made him appear suspicious to his former partner. They thought he'd become a witness in the smuggling case.

Gayle Leeson

I went into the kitchen where Jackie was solemnly chopping carrots. Putting my hand on her forearm, I said, "What happened to Devon was in no way your fault."

"I know." The tears glittering on her lashes contradicted her words.

"Belinda was a fool to not realize how much Devon loved her and to think he'd cheat on her. Even his business partner knew that was so inconceivable that it made more sense to believe he'd become a federal witness before he'd cheat on his wife."

"But what does everyone else think?" she asked.

"Chris—and everyone else, I imagine—thinks Belinda's rash behavior led to her husband's death. You were doing a sweet thing for a friend. Anyone who knows you would never think you'd break Roger's heart or destroy another person's home." I moved over to the grill. "I'm going to make Walter, Dilly, and Chris their breakfast. Then would you mind taking over for just a couple of minutes?"

"No problem."

A few minutes later, I put the three orders onto the window ledge for Scott to pick up, and I stepped outside with my smartphone. I logged onto social media and searched for *Richard D'Angelo*. Nothing matched the criteria of the man who'd served as Devon's partner. *Rick D'Angelo* was also a bust, but I hit pay dirt with *Ricky D'Angelo*. Not only did the man fit the description, he had *Devon Murphy* in his friends list.

Bingo.

Searching through Ricky D'Angelo's photos, I found a snapshot of Ricky and another man at the beach. The man looked familiar. I mentally removed his beard and made his face fuller. The profile tagged in the photo was that of *Neal D'Angelo*.

Jackie poked her head out the door. "Sorry, but I need your help. A church group just arrived."

Mom, Aunt Bess, and Clark arrived at around ten o'clock. Mom and Clark wore their *Down South Café* shirts, jeans, and jackets. Aunt Bess wore a red pant-suit with sequins on the lapels and had a little Santa hat perched on her head.

Homer wasn't far behind. Like Mom and Clark, he wore a *Down South Café* shirt and jeans.

"Good morning, Homer. Would you like me to go ahead and get your sausage biscuit ready?"

He glanced at the clock. "We have to be lined up for the parade at ten-thirty, right?"

"Right." That was the time he usually had his biscuit.

"We can get there in ten minutes," he said, "so I'll have my biscuit at 10:15 please. I'm flexible, but let's not go too crazy."

I pressed my lips together to keep from laughing and headed for the kitchen.

"Who's your hero today, Guru Guy?" Scott asked.

"Keanu Reeves, who once said that the simple act of paying attention can take you a long way."

I'd just delivered Homer's sausage biscuit when Ryan and his parents got to the café. I wanted to tell Ryan what I'd learned on social media, but I didn't really have time. Besides, I didn't want to spoil the fun he was having with his parents. Michelle was delighted with the cookies she'd made and proudly gave one to her husband and her son.

"Amy, your car looks super," Ryan's dad, David, said.

"Thank you. I—" I was interrupted by Ryan giving me a kiss on the cheek.

"Gotta run," he said. "I'm helping with traffic, crowd control, all that good stuff. I'll see you all after the parade, though."

"We should go get in line," Aunt Bess said. "We want a prominent spot."

Roger stepped into the café then. "Hey, Flowerpot, I checked the luggage rack to make sure it's good and sturdy."

Aunt Bess gave him a quick hug. "Thanks, dear, but we have to roll."

Jackie hurried over and kissed Aunt Bess's cheek. "We'll be watching for you when the parade comes by here."

"Scott, Homer, would you like to ride with Jenna and me?" Clark asked.

"Yes, sir." Scott grabbed two baskets of cookies to put in Clark's SUV.

Homer scrambled to finish his coffee and wipe his mouth on his napkin. "Oh, wait, I have to pay."

"It's on me this morning, Homer," I said. "It's my thank-you for helping hand out cookies."

"I don't need a thank you for that! I'm—"

"Well, you'll take it," Aunt Bess said. "I'm not going to be late to my parade."

We went outside and got into the car. Aunt Bess waved goodbye to everyone as if she was the homecoming queen. *My parade* indeed.

"See you along the parade route!" Michelle called.

As we slowly drove to the gathering spot, Aunt Bess practiced her wave.

"I've got the passenger side whipped," she said, "but I need a better wave for the people on the other side of the road."

"I'll be waving too, you know."

She frowned slightly. "You need to concentrate on driving and not running anyone over. That sweet little Scott will be walking right beside our car."

"So will my mother," I reminded her.

"Oh, yeah."

When we got to the meeting place, a woman in a puffy coat with a clipboard told us we were between the Winter Garden High School marching band and an ambulance.

I looked over at Aunt Bess. "Well, that's good news. If I'm waving at onlookers and accidentally hit Scott or Mom, help will be right behind us."

She was not amused.

At last, we started down Main Street. Admittedly, it was really cool to see all the people lining the street. Many of them were pointing at the cake and were happily accepting cookies from either Scott, Homer, Mom, or Clark. Our four volunteers seemed to be having a blast. Not as much as Aunt Bess, but then I doubted anyone was.

Could Aunt Bess's day get better, you ask? You wouldn't think so. But then it did.

As the parade turned off Main Street to go into a different part of town, I spotted Bryson Neal shoving Adam Tate into the back of a car. It looked as if Adam's hands were tied behind his back.

"Did you see that?" I asked Aunt Bess.

"That handsome fellow blowing me a kiss? Yessiree, Bob, I saw that!"

"No! Bryson Neal just pushed Adam Tate into a car!" I tried to control my breathing, so I didn't hyperventilate. "Aunt Bess, I believe that man killed Devon, and Adam might be next."

She went from catering to her adoring public to crime solver in two seconds flat. "How are we going to handle this?"

"He's turning onto Cyprus to take the shortcut back to the highway." I fumbled for my phone and handed it to her. "Pull up my contacts and call Ryan. We can't let Bryson get away."

When we got to Cyprus, I had a tough decision to make. Instead of going straight with the parade, we slowly turned and followed Bryson's car. The ambulance turned too.

Oops.

"Put Ryan on speaker when he answers please," I said.

She did so, and Ryan's voice filled the car.

"Hey, sweetheart, is everything all right?"

"No, it's not," Aunt Bess said. "Amy and I are in hot pursuit of a black sedan, license plate—I don't know because I can't see it."

"Is this a joke?" he asked.

"No," she said. "We're unarmed, and we need backup."

"Ryan, I think Bryson Neal is actually *Bryson Neal D'Angelo* and that he's related to Devon's partner," I said.

"We know. Belinda told us. She's terrified of the man." He blew out a breath. "Can you give me your exact location?"

"We're on Cyprus Road," I said.

"Where exactly?" he asked.

"We're in a yellow Bug with an enormous cake on the roof," Aunt Bess said. "We shouldn't be too hard to find!"

Bryson stopped at a railroad crossing.

"Oh, no." I groaned. "The train is coming. He knows we're behind him."

"Once again, we're hard to miss," Aunt Bess said.

Bryson got out of his car. He had a gun down by his side.

While I was screaming the play-by-play to Ryan, Aunt Bess was shouting, "Duck and floor it!"

I didn't duck, but I did reflexively hit the gas pedal. The car lurched forward. Slamming on the brakes to keep from hitting Bryson, I watched as my coffee cup top tier of the cake crashed down onto the man.

Bryson deflected the cake, but it provided the distraction Adam needed to get out of the back of the car and send Bryson sprawling. He hadn't knocked the gun from Bryson's hand though.

I slammed the gearshift into park and jumped out of the car just as Aunt Bess opened her door. "Don't you dare!" I ran forward and stepped onto Bryson's wrist to keep him from raising the gun.

"I'll kill you all! I swear I will!" he shouted.

Aunt Bess got out of the car and started snapping photos with her phone. "Live action shots for my *Crime Scenes* board! It doesn't get much better than this!"

As I stood there on Bryson's arm, I looked around and saw that not only was the train coming, but the ambulance had followed us...and so had the hardware store float...and the firetruck with Santa. Aunt Bess was right—it didn't get much better than that.

Epilogue

Jackie called me early Sunday morning. I'd been so tired that I'd gone back to bed after feeding Rory and Princess Eloise an hour earlier.

"What's going on?" I asked groggily, hoping she hadn't had a relapse of her illness.

"I'm at the café," she said. "I need you to come over here."

Immediately awake, I sat up in bed. "What's wrong?"

"Nothing. I—"

The phone went completely silent. Had Jackie muted the call, or had we been disconnected?

"Hello?" I asked. "Jackie, are you there?"

"Um, yeah, sorry. There's just something here you need to see."

I quickly got up and got dressed. Hurrying to the café, I saw that the parking lot was filled with familiar vehicles. I whipped my cosmetics case out of my purse and made myself presentable before going into the building.

Taking a deep breath, I got out of the Bug—now without the cake topper, which had been removed by Roger and Ryan yesterday evening—and walked toward the door.

Unable to stand it, Jackie opened the door and shouted, "Surprise!"

"Why? What's the occasion?"

She laughed. "You're a celebrity." Tugging my arm, she pulled me into the café where I was greeted with cheers and applause.

"Aw, come on," I said. "This is totally unnecessary."

"No, it isn't." Jackie nodded toward Scott. "Our favorite wild child and I prepared a brunch buffet, so you don't have to do any work today. Simply relax and enjoy being with friends and family."

In addition to her and Scott, Roger, Ryan, Aunt Bess, Mom, Clark, Homer, Dilly, Walter, Michelle and David Hall, Ivy and a man I guessed to be Ivy's husband were gathered in the dining room.

"Look!" Aunt Bess pointed to framed photographs of newspaper articles showcasing the Bug in yesterday's parade adorning several of the tables. "I'm featured prominently in most of the pictures, but don't let that take away from your part in our heroic actions."

I laughed.

Mom came over and gave me a hug. "I was proud of you for simply creating the float but seeing the headline *Local Café's Giant Cake Float Helps Thwart Killer* absolutely made my year."

"Thanks." I checked out each of the articles, not realizing how much press had been generated by the parade's part in capturing Brandon Neal.

Scott's sister Ivy sidled next to me. Her auburn hair was pulled into a French braid, and she wore a denim shirtdress. "You—and everyone else here in this dining room—have meant the world to Scott. I appreciate everything you're doing for him."

"I'm grateful for everything he does for us," I said. "He's going to be—" I gulped.

She smiled. "He told me he let it slip. And, yes, he's going to be a wonderful uncle." She motioned someone over. "Amy, I'd like you to meet my husband, Matt."

Matt was tall with an athletic build and a military bearing. I knew he was in the armed services, but I hadn't realized he was home on leave.

"It's a pleasure to meet you," I told him. "Ivy and Scott are the best. You're blessed to have them in your family."

"Don't I know it," he said. "It's nice to meet you too, Amy."

We chatted for a few minutes, and then Ryan joined me.

"Do you have any idea how busy you're going to be tomorrow?" he asked. "The café is famous now."

I scoffed. "Hardly."

"Don't be such a skeptic." He spread his hands. "You helped capture a murderer, allowed Belinda to be bold enough to testify in a federal smuggling operation, and showed off your cake decorating prowess. That's impressive stuff."

"How did Belinda not know Sheila was dating Richard D'Angelo?" I asked.

He shrugged. "She thinks Sheila probably didn't tell her because D'Angelo was threatening Devon."

Homer walked by with a sausage biscuit on a plate.

"Homer, who's your hero today?" I asked him.

"You are." He smiled. "You're all of Winter Garden's hero today."

Acknowledgements

Thank you so very much to Rosemary Galpin, Master Sugar Artist at Texas Home Baker in Luling, Texas. When I asked Rosemary if it would be possible to make and anchor a large dummy cake onto the top of a Volkswagen Beetle, she went above and beyond in providing instructions. She started with the cake board Amy would need and walked me through the process step-by-step. If you want to see some gorgeous creations, please look for Rosemary on Facebook and Twitter—or Google her to see her award-winning creations featured in the media.

Recipes from the Down South Café

Easiest Candy Ever

Ingredients
1 can sweetened condensed milk
1 12-oz. pkg. of chocolate chips (semi-sweet or milk – your preference)
1 12-oz. pkg. of peanut butter chips (you can also substitute mint chips)

In a saucepan, combine your milk and chocolate chips. Stir until chips are melted. Remove the saucepan from heat and stir in the peanut butter chips. Pour into an 8 x 8-inch baking pan lined with aluminum foil. Put the pan into the refrigerator. After the candy has set (about an hour or two), take the candy out of the pan and peel the foil from the back. Cut into squares.

Yield: 64 1-inch pieces

Tiramisu Bundt Cake

Ingredients
1 (18-oz.) box white cake mix
1 pint coffee ice cream, melted
3 eggs
1 12-oz. container of whipped vanilla frosting
1 teaspoon instant coffee granules dissolved in 1 tablespoon water
Cinnamon sugar for dusting (optional)

Preheat the oven to 350°F (180°C, Gas Mark 4). Coat a 10-cup Bundt pan with non-stick cooking spray. In large bowl, beat the cake mix, melted ice cream, and eggs on low speed for one minute. Beat for 2 minutes on medium speed. Pour batter into prepared pan. Bake for 35 to 40 minutes, or until a wooden pick inserted into the center of the cake comes out clean. Cool in the pan on a wire rack for 20 minutes. Invert the pan onto wire rack to cool completely. In large bowl, beat together the frosting and instant coffee mixture. Spread the frosting onto the cake in an even layer. Dust with cinnamon sugar, if desired. Refrigerate until ready to serve.

Yield: 8-10 servings

*If you like these recipes, they and several others are in *Tea For You*, a complimentary e-book of recipes based on the Victoria Square Mysteries and the Life On Victoria Square companion series which I co-write with Lorraine Bartlett. To download the e-book, visit me at http://www.gayleleeson.com and click the *Victoria Square Series* tab.

Also by Gayle Leeson

Down South Café Mystery Series

The Calamity Café

Silence of the Jams

Honey-Baked Homicide

Apples and Alibis

Ghostly Fashionista Mystery Series

Designs on Murder

Perils and Lace

Kinsey Falls Chick-Lit Series

Hightail It to Kinsey Falls

Putting Down Roots in Kinsey Falls

Sleighing It in Kinsey Falls

Victoria Square Series (With Lorraine Bartlett)

Yule Be Dead

Murder Ink

Murderous Misconception

Embroidery Mystery Series (Written as Amanda Lee)

The Quick and The Thread

Stitch Me Deadly

Thread Reckoning

The Long Stitch Goodnight

Thread on Arrival

Cross-Stitch Before Dying

Thread End

Wicked Stitch

The Stitching Hour

Better Off Thread

Cake Decorating Mystery Series (Written as Gayle Trent)

Murder Takes the Cake

Dead Pan

Killer Sweet Tooth

Battered to Death

Killer Wedding Cake

Myrtle Crumb Mystery Series (Written as Gayle Trent)

The Party Line (short story/prequel)

Between A Clutch and a Hard Place

When Good Bras Go Bad

Claus of Death

Soup...Er...Myrtle!

Perp and Circumstance

ABOUT THE AUTHOR

Gayle Leeson is known for her cozy mysteries. She also writes as Gayle Trent and Amanda Lee. To eliminate confusion going forward, Gayle is writing under the name Gayle Leeson only. She and her family live in Southwest Virginia with Cooper, the Great Pyrenees in the photograph with Gayle, and a small pride of lions (cats, really, but humor them).

If you enjoyed this book, Gayle would appreciate your leaving a review. If you don't know what to say, there is a handy book review guide at her site (https://www.gayleleeson.com/book-review-form). Gayle invites you to sign up for her newsletter and receive excerpts of some of her books: https://forms.aweber.com/form/14/1780369214.htm

Social Media Links:
Twitter:

https://twitter.com/GayleTrent

Facebook:

https://www.facebook.com/GayleLeeson/

BookBub:

https://www.bookbub.com/profile/gayle-leeson

Goodreads:

https://www.goodreads.com/author/show/426208.Gayle_Trent

Have You Met Max, the Ghostly Fashionista?

Excerpt from *Designs on Murder*

Chapter One

A flash of brilliant light burst from the lower righthand window of Shops on Main, drawing my attention to the FOR LEASE sign. I'd always loved the building and couldn't resist going inside to see the space available.

I opened the front door to the charming old mansion, which had started life as a private home in the late 1800s and had had many incarnations since then. I turned right to open another door to go into the vacant office.

"Why so glum, chum?" asked a tall, attractive woman with a dark brown bob and an impish grin. She stood near the window wearing a rather fancy mauve gown for the middle of the day. She was also wearing a headband with a peacock feather, making her look like a flapper from the 1920s. I wondered if she might be going to some sort of party after work. Either that, or this woman was quite the eccentric.

"I just came from a job interview," I said.

"Ah. Don't think it went well, huh?"

"Actually, I think it did. But I'm not sure I want to be doing that kind of work for...well...forever."

"Nothing's forever, darling. But you've come to the right place. My name's Max, by the way. Maxine, actually, but I hate that stuffy old name. Maxine Englebright. Isn't that a mouthful? You can see why I prefer Max."

I chuckled. "It's nice to meet you, Max. I'm Amanda Tucker."

"So, Amanda Tucker," Max said, moving over to the middle of the room, "what's your dream job?"

"I know it'll sound stupid. I shouldn't have even wandered in here--"

"Stop that please. Negativity gets us nowhere."

Max sounded like a school teacher then, and I tried to assess her age. Although she somehow seemed older, she didn't look much more than my twenty-four years. I'd put her at about thirty...if that. Since she was looking at me expectantly, I tried to give a better answer to her question.

"I want to fill a niche...to make some sort of difference," I said. "I want to do something fun, exciting...something I'd look forward to doing every day."

"And you're considering starting your own business?"

"That was my initial thought upon seeing that this space is for lease. I love this building...always have."

"What sort of business are you thinking you'd like to put here?" Max asked.

"I enjoy fashion design, but my parents discouraged me because—they said—it was as hard to break into as professional sports. I told them there are a lot of people in professional sports, but they said, 'Only the best, Mandy.'"

Max gave an indignant little bark. "Oh, that's hooey! But I can identify. My folks never thought I'd amount to much. Come to think of it, I guess I didn't." She threw back her head and laughed.

"Oh, well, I wish I could see some of your designs."

"You can. I have a couple of my latest right here on my phone." I took my cell phone from my purse and pulled up the two designs I'd photographed the day before. The first dress had a small pink and green floral print on a navy background, shawl collar, three-quarter length sleeves, and A-line skirt. "I love vintage styles."

"This is gorgeous! I'd love to have a dress like this."

"Really?"

"Yeah. What else ya got?" Max asked.

My other design was an emerald 1930s-style bias cut evening gown with a plunging halter neckline and a back panel with pearl buttons that began at the middle of the back on each side and went to the waist.

Max caught her breath. "That's the berries, kid!"

"Thanks." I could feel the color rising in my cheeks. Max might throw out some odd phrases, but I could tell she liked the dress. "Mom and Dad are probably right, though. Despite the fact that I use modern fabrics—some with quirky, unusual patterns—how could I be sure I'd have the clientele to actually support a business?"

"Are you kidding me? People would love to have their very own fashion designer here in little ol' Abingdon."

"You really think so? Is it the kind of place you'd visit?" I asked.

"Visit?" Max laughed. "Darling, I'd practically live in it."

"All right. I'll think about it."

"Think quickly please. There was someone in here earlier today looking at the space. He wants to sell cigars and tobacco products. Pew. The smell would drive me screwy. I'd much rather have you here."

Hmm...the lady had her sales pitch down. I had to give her that. "How much is the rent?"

"Oh, I have no idea. You'll find Mrs. Meacham at the top of the stairs, last door on your left. It's marked OFFICE."

"Okay. I'll go up and talk with her."

"Good luck, buttercup!"

I was smiling and shaking my head as I mounted the stairs. Max was a character. I thought she'd be a fun person to have around.

Since the office wasn't a retail space like the other rooms in the building, I knocked and waited for a response before entering.

Mrs. Meacham was a plump, prim woman with short, curly white hair and sharp blue eyes. She looked at me over the top of her reading glasses. "How may I help you?"

"I'm interested in the space for rent downstairs," I said.

"You are? Oh, my! I thought you were here selling cookies or something. You look so young." Mrs. Meacham laughed at her own joke, so I faked a chortle to be polite. "What type of shop are you considering?"

"A fashion boutique."

"Fashion?"

"Yes, I design and create retro-style fashions."

"Hmm. I never picked up sewing myself. I've never been big on crafts." She stood and opened a file cabinet to the left of her desk, and I could see she was wearing a navy suit. "Canning and baking were more my strengths. I suppose you could say I prefer the kitchen to the hearth." She laughed again, and I chuckled along with her.

She turned and handed me an application. "Just read this over and call me back if you have any questions. If you're interested in the space, please let me know as soon as possible. There's a gentleman interested in opening a cigar store there." She tapped a pen on her desk blotter. "But even if he gets here before you do, we'll have another opening by the first of the month. The web designer across the hall is leaving. Would you like to take a look at his place before you decide?"

"No, I'd really prefer the shop on the ground floor," I said.

"All right. Well, I hope to hear from you soon."

I left then. I stopped back by the space for lease to say goodbye to Max, but she was gone.

I went home—my parents' home actually, but they moved to Florida for Dad's job more than two years ago, so it was basically mine...until they wanted it back. I made popcorn for lunch, read over Mrs. Meacham's contract, and started crunching the numbers.

I'd graduated in May with a bachelor's degree in business administration with a concentration in marketing and entrepreneurship but just couldn't find a position that sparked any sort of passion in me.

This morning I'd had yet another interview where I'd been overqualified for the position but felt I had a good chance of getting an offer...a low offer...for work I couldn't see myself investing decades doing.

Jasmine, my cat, wandered into the room. She'd eaten some kibble from her bowl in the kitchen and was now interested in what I was having. She hopped onto the coffee table, peeped into the popcorn bowl, and turned away dismissively to clean her paws. She was a beautiful gray and white striped tabby. Her feet were white, and she looked as if she were wearing socks of varying lengths—crew socks on the back, anklets on the front.

"What do you think, Jazzy?" I asked. "Should I open a fashion boutique?"

She looked over her shoulder at me for a second before resuming her paw-licking. I didn't know if that was a yes or a no.

Even though I'd gone to school for four years to learn all about how to open, manage, and provide inventory for a small business, I researched for the remainder of the afternoon. I checked out the stats on independent designers in the United States and fashion boutiques in Virginia. There weren't many in the Southwest Virginia region, so I knew I'd have something unique to offer my clientele.

Finally, Jazzy let me know that she'd been napping long enough and that we needed to do something. Mainly, I needed to feed her again, and she wanted to eat. But I had other ideas.

"Jazzy, let's get your carrier. You and I are going to see Grandpa Dave."

Grandpa Dave was my favorite person on the planet, and Jazzy thought pretty highly of him herself. He lived only about ten minutes away from us. He was farther out in the country and had a bigger home than we did. Jazzy and I were happy in our little three-bedroom, one bath ranch. We secretly hoped Dad wouldn't lose the job that had taken him and Mom to Florida and that they'd love it too much to leave when he retired because we'd gotten used to having the extra space.

I put the carrier on the backseat of my green sedan. It was a cute car that I'd worked the summer between high school and college to get enough money to make the down payment on, but it felt kinda ironic to be driving a cat around in a car that reminded people of a hamster cage.

Sometimes, I wished my Mom and Dad's house was a bit farther from town. It was so peaceful out here in the country. Fences, pastureland, and cows bordered each side of the road. There were a few houses here and there, but most of the land was still farmland. The farmhouses were back off the road and closer to the barns.

When we pulled into Grandpa Dave's long driveway, Jazzy meowed.

"Yes," I told her. "We're here."

Grandpa Dave lived about fifty yards off the road, and his property was fenced, but he didn't keep any animals. He'd turned the barn that had been on the land when he and Grandma Jodie bought it into a workshop where he liked to "piddle."

I pulled around to the side of the house and was happy to see that, rather than piddling in the workshop, Grandpa was sitting on one of the white rocking chairs on the porch. I parked and got out, opened the door to both the car and the carrier for Jazzy, and she ran straight to hop onto his lap.

"Well, there's my girls!" Grandpa Dave laughed.

It seemed to me that Grandpa was almost always laughing. He'd lost a little of that laughter after Grandma Jodie had died. But that was five years ago, and, except for some moments of misty remembrance, he was back to his old self.

I gave him a hug and a kiss on the cheek before settling onto the swing.

"I was sorta expecting you today," he said. "How'd the interview go?"

"It went fine, I guess, but I'm not sure Integrated Manufacturing Technologies is for me. The boss was nice, and the offices are beautiful, but...I don't know."

"What ain't she telling me, Jazzy?"

The cat looked up at him adoringly before butting her head against his chin.

"I'm...um...I'm thinking about starting my own business." I didn't venture a glance at Grandpa Dave right away. I wasn't sure I wanted to know what he was thinking. I figured he was thinking I'd come to ask for money--which I had, money and advice—but I was emphatic it was going to be a loan.

Grandpa had already insisted on paying my college tuition and wouldn't hear of my paying him back. This time, I was giving him no choice in the matter. Either he'd lend me the money, and sign the loan agreement I'd drafted, or I wouldn't take it.

I finally raised my eyes to look at his face, and he was looking pensive.

"Tell me what brought this on," he said.

I told him about wandering into Shops on Main after my interview and meeting Maxine Englebright. "She loved the designs I showed her and seemed to think I could do well if I opened a boutique there. I went upstairs and got an application from the building manager, and then I went home and did some research. I'd never seriously considered opening my own business before--at least, not at this stage of my career--but I'd like to try."

Another glance at Grandpa Dave told me he was still listening but might take more convincing.

"I realize I'm young, and I'm aware that more than half of all small businesses fail in the first four years. But I've got a degree that says I'm qualified to manage a business. Why not manage my own?"

He remained quiet.

"I know that opening a fashion boutique might seem frivolous, but there aren't a lot of designers in this region. I believe I could fill a need...or at least a niche."

Grandpa sat Jazzy onto the porch and stood. Without a word, he went into the house.

Jazzy looked up at me. *Meow?* She went over to the door to see where Grandpa Dave went. *Meow?* She stood on her hind legs and peered through the door.

"Watch out, Jasmine," he said, waiting for her to hop down and back away before he opened the door.

He was carrying his checkbook. "How much do you need?"

"Well, I have some savings, and—"

"That's not what I asked."

"Okay. Now, this will be a loan, Grandpa Dave, not a gift."

"If you don't tell me how much, I'm taking this checkbook back into the house, and we won't discuss it any further."

"Ten thousand dollars," I blurted.

As he was writing the check, he asked, "Have you and Jazzy had your dinner yet?"

We were such frequent guests that he kept her favorite cat food on hand.

"We haven't. Do you have the ingredients to make a pizza?"

He scoffed. "Like I'm ever without pizza-makings." He handed me the check. "By the way, how old is this Max you met today? She sounds like quite a gal."

"She doesn't look all that much older than me. But she seems more worldly...or something. I think you'd like her," I said. "But wait, aren't you still seeing Betsy?"

He shrugged. "Betsy is all right to take to Bingo...but this Max sounds like she could be someone special."

First thing the next morning, I went to the bank to set up a business account for Designs on You. That's what I decided to name my shop. Then I went to Shops on Main and gave Mrs. Meacham my application. After she made sure everything was in order, she took my check for the first month's rent and then took me around to meet the rest of the shop owners.

She introduced me to the upstairs tenants first. There was Janice, who owned Janice's Jewelry. She was of average height but she wore stilettos, had tawny hair with blonde highlights, wore a shirt that was way too tight, and was a big fan of dermal fillers, given her expressionless face.

"Janice, I'd like you to meet Amanda," said Mrs. Meacham. "She's going to be opening a fashion boutique downstairs."

"Fashion? You and I should talk, Amanda. You dress them, and I'll accessorize them." She giggled before turning to pick up a pendant with a large, light green stone. "With your coloring, you'd look lovely in one of these Amazonite necklace and earring sets."

"I'll have to check them out later," I said. "It was nice meeting you."

Janice grabbed a stack of her business cards and pressed them into my hand. "Here. For your clients. I'll be glad to return the favor."

"Great. Thanks."

Next, Mrs. Meacham took me to meet Mark, a web site designer. Everything about Mark screamed thin. The young man didn't appear to have an ounce of fat on his body. He had thinning black hair. He wore a thin crocheted tie. He held out a thin hand for me to shake. His handshake was surprisingly firm.

"Hello. It's a pleasure to meet you, Amanda." He handed me a card from the holder on his desk. "Should you need any web design help or marketing expertise, please call on me. I can work on a flat fee or monthly fee basis, depending on your needs."

"Thank you, but—"

"Are you aware that fifty percent of fledgling businesses fail within the first year?" he asked.

I started to correct his stats, but I didn't want to alienate someone I was going to be working near. I thanked him again and told him I appreciated his offer. It dawned on me as Mrs. Meacham and I were moving on to the next tenant that she'd said the web designer was leaving at the end of the month...which was only a week away. I wondered where he was taking his business.

The other upstairs shop was a bookstore called Antiquated Editions. The owner was a burly, bearded man who'd have looked more at home in a motorcycle shop than selling rare books, but, hey, you can't judge a book by its cover, right?

I made a mental note to tell Grandpa Dave my little joke. As you've probably guessed, I didn't have a lot of friends. Not that I wasn't a friendly person. I had a lot of acquaintances. It was just hard for me to get close to people. I wasn't the type to tell my deepest, darkest secrets to someone I hadn't known...well, all my life.

The brawny book man's name was Ford. I'd have been truly delighted had it been Harley, but had you been expecting me to say his name was Fitzgerald or Melville, please see the aforementioned joke about books and covers. He was friendly and invited me to come around and look at his collection anytime. I promised I'd do so after I got settled in.

Then it was downstairs to meet the rest of the shop owners. The first shop on the left when you came in the door--the shop directly across the hall from mine--was Delightful Home. The proprietress was Connie, who preferred a hug over a handshake.

"Aren't you lovely?" Connie asked.

I did not say I doubt it, which was the first thought that popped into my brain, but I did thank her for the compliment. Connie was herself the embodiment of lovely. She had long, honey blonde hair that she wore in a single braid. Large silver hoops adorned her ears, and she had skinny silver bracelets stacked up each arm. She wore an embroidered red tunic that fell to her thighs, black leggings, and Birkenstocks. But the thing that made her truly lovely wasn't so much her looks but the way she appeared to boldly embrace life. I mean, the instant we met, she embraced me. Her shop smelled of cinnamon and something else...sage, maybe.

"Melba, that blue is definitely your color," Connie said. "By the way, did that sinus blend help you?"

"It did!" Mrs. Meacham turned to me. "Connie has the most wonderful products, not the least of which are her essential oils."

I could see that Connie had an assortment of candles, soaps, lotions, oils, and tea blends. I was curious to see what all she did have, but that would have to wait.

"I'm here to help you in any way I possibly can," said Connie, with a warm smile. "Anything you need, just let me know. We're neighbors now."

Mrs. Meacham took me to meet the last of my "neighbors," Mr. and Mrs. Peterman.

"Call us Ella and Frank," Ella insisted. She was petite with salt-and-pepper hair styled in a pixie cut.

Frank was average height, had a slight paunch, a bulbous nose, and bushy brown hair. He didn't say much.

Ella and Frank had a paper shop. They designed their own greeting cards and stationery, and they sold specialty and novelty items that would appeal to their clientele. For instance, they had socks with book patterns, quotes from famous books, and likenesses of authors.

After I'd met everyone, Mrs. Meacham handed me the keys to my shop and went upstairs. Although my shop wouldn't open until the first of September, she'd graciously given me this last week of August to get everything set up.

I unlocked my door and went inside. I was surprised to see Max standing by the window. I started to ask her how she'd got in, but then I saw that there was another door that led to the kitchen. I imagined my space had once been the family dining room. Anyway, it was apparent that the door between my space and the kitchen hallway had been left unlocked. I'd have to be careful to check that in the future.

But, for now, I didn't mind at all that Max was there. Or that it appeared she was wearing the same outfit she'd been wearing yesterday. Must have been some party!

"So, you leased the shop?" Max asked.

"I did!"

"Congratulations! I wish we could have champagne to celebrate."

I laughed. "Me too, but I'm driving."

Max joined in my laughter. "I'm so glad you're going to be here. I think we'll be great friends."

"I hope so." And I truly did. I immediately envisioned Max as my best friend—the two of us going to lunch together, talking about guys and clothes, shopping together. I reined myself in before I got too carried away.

I surveyed the room. The inside wall to my right had a fireplace. I recalled that all the rooms upstairs had them too. But this one had built-in floor-to-ceiling bookshelves on either side of the fireplace.

"Does this fireplace still work?" I asked Max.

"I imagine it would, but it isn't used anymore. The owners put central heat and air in eons ago."

"Just checking. I mean, I wasn't going to light fire to anything. I merely wanted to be sure it was safe to put flammables on these shelves." I could feel my face getting hot. "I'm sorry. That was a stupid thing to say. I'm just so excited—"

"And I'm excited for you. You have nothing to apologize for. How were you supposed to know whether or not the former tenant ever lit the fireplace?"

"You're really nice."

"And you're too hard on yourself. Must you be brilliant and well-spoken all the time?"

"Well...I'm certainly not, but I'd like to be."

"Tell me what you have in store for this place," she said.

I indicated the window. "I'd like to have a table flanked by chairs on either side here." I bit my lip. "Where's the best place around here to buy some reasonably priced furniture that would go with the overall atmosphere of the building?"

"I have no idea. You should ask Connie."

"Connie?" I was actually checking to make sure I'd heard Max correctly, but it so happened that I'd left the door open and Connie was walking by as I spoke.

"Yes?"

"Max was telling me that you might know of a good furniture place nearby," I said.

"Max?" Connie looked about the room. "Who's Max?"

I whirled around, thinking Max had somehow slipped out of the room. But, nope, there she stood...shaking her head...and putting a finger to her lips.

"Um...she was....she was just here. She was here yesterday too. I assumed she was a Shops on Main regular."

"I don't know her, but I'd love to meet her some-time. As for the furniture, I'd try the antique stores downtown for starters. You might fall in love with just the right piece or two there." She grinned. "I'd better get back to minding the store. Good luck with the furniture shopping!"

Connie pulled the door closed behind her as she left, and I was glad. I turned to Max.

"Gee, that was awkward," she said. "I was sure you knew."

"Knew?"

"That I'm a ghost."

Interested in reading more? Designs on Murder, Book One in the Ghostly Fashionista Mystery Series, only 99 cents - www.ghostlyfashionista.com